not in the diary

not in the diary

THORA HIRD

WITH LIZ BARR

Hodder & Stoughton
LONDON SYDNEY AUCKLAND

British Library Cataloguing in Publication Data
A record for this book is available from the British Library

ISBN 0 340 74619 X

Typeset by Avon Dataset Ltd, Bidford-on-Avon, Warks

Printed and bound in Great Britain by
Clays Ltd, St Ives plc

Hodder & Stoughton Ltd
A Division of Hodder Headline
338 Euston Road
London NW1 3BH

Contents

Foreword

I'm delighted to be writing the foreword to this book, partly because I'm a huge fan of Thora's work, books and performances, and partly because if I wasn't writing this I'd be in the kitchen getting Puffed Wheat off the table mats. Which is alright once in a while but I wouldn't want to make a habit of it.

I have been an admirer of Thora since the days of *Meet the Wife* and *First Lady*, but our paths didn't cross professionally till a few years ago. I first worked with her in 1994 when she played Duncan Preston's mother in the BBC Screen One *Pat and Margaret*. I had written to her ten years earlier when I was doing my sketch show *As Seen On TV*, but 1994 was the first year she had free.

We were on a very tight schedule for *Pat and Margaret*, and the second day that Thora was to be with us was threatened by industrial action. Nobody wanted to break the strike, due to begin at 9 a.m., but we couldn't afford to lose a day with Thora either. Thora solved the problem. She agreed to film all her scenes very early in the morning, and she had them all in the can by nine o'clock. In one scene she is told by her son, Jim, that not only has he had a sex life with his girlfriend, Margaret, played by me, but that he has had it in his mother's bed. Thora recoiled as only she can: 'Not on the eiderdown?'

The film was known ever after among the crew as the 'Not on the Eiderdown' show, and I have an enduring mental picture of little Thora in her pinny, dusting her front gate and doing things with a feather duster that were definitely post-watershed.

The second time we worked together was in 1998, on *Dinnerladies*. I had had an idea for one of the episodes that the mothers of all the dinnerladies should visit the canteen and spread alarm, embarrassment and mayhem. My mother was of course Julie Walters, so I couldn't pair myself off with Thora and instead donated her to Thelma Barlow, playing the prim and slim Dolly. Dora Brien was Anne Reid's mother and Eric Sykes played the ex-Desert Rat father of Duncan Preston's Stan. As Thora says in the book, Eric had lots of ideas about how he wanted to play the part, some of which I agreed with and some I didn't, and it was quite exciting on the night waiting to see which way he would plunge. Thora had to embarrass the recently slimmed-down Dolly by explaining to the assembled company how Dolly had looked in years gone by: 'She was a lovely child, dainty, like a little doll, then woof, she was like a dinghy with plaits.'

It was lovely having Thora in these two shows, but we still wanted to do something together, so when the BBC asked me to contribute to their millennium sketch show, it was the perfect opportunity to write a two-hander. The brief was comedy through the ages, but I ignored that and wrote a sketch set in a hairdressers, with me as the flustered stylist who comes downstairs to find her ex-husband has scrawled offensive remarks all over the loose covers in Marmite. As she points out, it must have taken him ages: 'It doesn't flow, Marmite, it's not like Golden Syrup in that regard . . .'

Bearing in mind that we would have very little rehearsal time, I kept Thora's lines to a minimum, and just gave her the tag. Back came the word from Hird: could she have more dialogue please. I don't know, you'd think being an icon, a dame and a treasure would be enough for some people, but Thora wants to get laughs as well. Luckily for us all, she gets them.

Victoria Wood

Introduction

When the publishers approached me for another book – a third volume of autobiography – I told them I would rather write stories for children. They said they might want that later, but for now they wanted me to put down everything that had been happening to me during the last years of my life and call it *'It's in the Diary'*. (I don't mean the *last* years of my life. I mean the two or three years just past.)

I was eighty-five when I completed my second volume of autobiography in 1995, so you could be forgiven for thinking that it would be my last. But life goes on even when you are well over eighty – and rather a lot of things have happened to me since then. There have been three more years of *Last of the Summer Wine*. I played Violet in 'Waiting for the Telegram' for Alan Bennett's award winning *Talking Heads* television series and won the BAFTA for it, as well as being given four other awards – all in my eighty-ninth year. Then I played the lead in Derek Longden's wonderful play about his mother, *Lost for Words*. I've also been made Vice-president of Help the Aged. So there are a few things worth the telling.

But at my age, you can't tell your story about *now*,

1

without explaining about *then*. I learned how to act by playing Cockney charladies and downstairs maids in Morecambe rep, and I could show you fifty-seven varieties of how to carry on a tray of coffee . . . and get a laugh. I learned my craft in the years I spent doing summer seasons – twice nightly at Blackpool – when Ken Dodd filled one theatre, Morecambe and Wise another, the Crazy Gang another, Arthur Askey another, and moi another. I learned from working with leading ladies of the West End in the forties, when leading ladies were very powerful figures indeed, the likes of Fay Compton and Gladys Cooper. If you got a laugh where they didn't want you to get a laugh, or you crossed them in any way, you could be sacked. I learned my craft in the early days at Ealing Studios, playing Dirk Bogarde's mother and Will Hay's secretary. What I'm saying is that the old friends and the old directors and performers, some long dead now, are all still part of any success I am having today.

So I said that I'd write this book – but only if I could call it 'Not *in the Diary*'. I said, 'There's more to my life than a collection of diary entries like, *13 January. Meet Alan Bennett for tea.*'

So they agreed, and here it is.

I've always enjoyed telling stories, and writing about my life, even when I was a little girl. Of course, I do it all by hand still. We have got one of those things everybody uses nowadays, a computer . . . in the cupboard. I remember my late husband Jimmy (James Scott, also known as Scottie) coming home with it one day, very proud. It's still in its box. Never been opened. My son-in-law, William, Jan's husband, took me up to his study one day. He said, 'All you have to do is . . .' At the end of the afternoon of him showing me all about everything I said, 'William. It's no good. I still don't know what to push. I'll just write it, if you don't mind.'

I was top of the class for writing essays at school. I have always been interested in history, and what I liked best was writing about people I knew in Morecambe and, when I could discover it, about my own family history. I had some colourful material to work with. My granddad, William Hird, my father's father, born in 1846, was – I think you could call him – a pirate. Red hair, red beard. He had his own schooner, and the only sad thing is that I don't have an oil painting of him. There was one, wrapped up in brown paper. I can remember it vividly. It was my granddaughter Daisy to the life, but a man. In the main bedroom in Morecambe houses there was a little space, almost like a cave, under the stairs that went up from the first landing to the top floor. And this portrait was kept there, wrapped up in brown paper. My mother was always saying, 'Great. We must find somewhere to put that.' But she never knew where it should go, so it never was hung. Many years later Lily, my sister-in-law, chucked it out when she cleaned up the house after my dad died.

It was a thing in the family was this, because you'd only to mention Granddad, and my father would say, 'If he walked through that door, I'd bloody shoot him.'

And we used to say, 'What with, Dad?'

'Never mind what with. I'd shoot him.'

Granddad used to go to sea – he was a sea-trader. He had always promised my grandmother that he would give it all up and settle down to work in the mills, but there was always 'one last one' before he gave it up. And then one day he disappeared. Nobody knew what had happened to him, and for years we thought he might just walk back in one day. (Whereupon my father would have shot him.)

There was a man in Morecambe called Mr Spencer, who lived in Graham Street. He was an old professor, or at least we thought he was a professor because he had so many books. We loved to go in his little house, because one whole room was all shelves of books. He came round to our house one teatime. Knocked on the front door.

'Are you there, James?' He always called my father James.

'Oh, come in, Mr Spencer.'

'I think you'll find this of great interest.'

He had a thick book with him, like a family Bible, green. I can see it now, with a piece of paper poked out of it. He said, 'I think you'll find this most interesting. Oh, good evening, Mrs Hird. May I just read this to you?'

It was all about the discovery of an abandoned ship in a bay in the South China Sea. Granddad's schooner. They knew to whom it had belonged from the brassbound logbook, with the name of the captain, Captain William Hird. There was no sign of the crew, but they gathered from local stories that they had all been hanged by their toes . . . for piracy.

After that we rather swanked about him. 'My grandfather, the buccaneer.' When my grandmother died, my father got the oil painting. It's really a shame Lily threw it out. And there was a beautiful oil painting of my mother, when she was fifteen. That's gone. My mother lived to see me courted and married to my darling Scottie, and she lived to see Janette born and helped me to look after her when she was a beautiful baby, so she must have known that I would have a happy life. But she died before I had any real professional success, and I never earned enough money in time to buy her things to make her own life a bit easier. That has been my greatest regret.

I've been very lucky, and I've got on, but the sad part has been not having my parents see me get on. They, more than anybody, taught me everything I know about the theatre. I would have loved them to have seen how I have been able to use all the things they instilled in me, and still do use them. My father said to me once, in front of the entire company, during rehearsals for *The Student Prince*, which he was directing, 'Do you know how to spell the word "comedienne", Miss Hird?'

I said, 'Yes, I think so.'

He said, 'Really. Only I wondered if you even knew what it meant.'

I know eighty-eight might be a bit late for saying, 'Look, Mum! Look, Dad! I've won the BAFTA!' But the sad thing is, they didn't really see any of it. Or did they? Are they still watching over me from somewhere?

My father did come to London to see me in *Flowers for the Living* after my mother had died. It wasn't in the West End, but still – a far cry from Morecambe rep. He came to stay with Scottie and me in our mews house in London, where I still live, and that night after seeing the play, just as he was going to bed, he did something very unlike him. He was standing by the sitting-room door ready to make an exit – he always 'made an exit', my dad. He never just left a room. I can see the exact spot where he was standing from where I'm sitting now, when he stood by the door and said, 'Goodnight, love. You're a wonderful bloody actress. I've *lived* to see you perform the way you did tonight.'

He taught me everything I know about comedy timing, my dad, and he had always taken a great interest in my work and criticised my performances and given me hints on how to improve them – but this was the first time he had *ever* praised me. He loved me, but he wasn't a man to give praise.

So that night, it was a big moment for me. But all I said was, 'Oh! Goodnight, Dad, God bless.' He gave me a little nod and went off to bed. The next morning when I took him his cup of tea, he was dead.

These things come back to you, you see. Whatever I am now, is because of what I was then. Do you follow my meaning? I'm as busy these days as I have ever been, and I'm very grateful for it. There are a lot of things in the diary still to do, if God spares me. Whether he will . . . that's *not* in the diary.

'But it's not home'

January 1998

27 January 12.00 Stuart Burge
(Director, 'Waiting for the Telegram')

From the end of 1997 and all during the early months of 1998 I was preparing for my roles in two major television dramas. In one I was to play an old lady of ninety-something, who was in a home, and in the other a lady of seventy-something, not in a home, but with Alzheimer's. It's an interesting sign of the times that in each case the 'old lady' role was also the leading role. And in the case of the Alan Bennett *Talking Heads* play, 'Waiting for the Telegram', it was the only role – because it was a monologue.

Now I'm eighty-eight. I'll be eighty-nine by the time you read this, God willing. But each time – this is true what I'm telling you – I thought to myself, 'Well, I've opened a lot of nursing homes and old people's homes, and I always make time to sit down with one or two of them and have a few words. I'll remember the things they say and how they said them. That'll help me think how to play it.'

Because – and this may sound a bit funny – I mean

funny strange, not funny tee-hee – I never think of *myself* as being old. I never think, 'Oh dear! That's a lot of words to learn at eighty-eight' or anything like that. In fact, I like to do what I can to help old people.

I've been made Vice-president of Help the Aged, and I did a little television interview some time ago at lunch-time. The television interviewer was a very good-looking young fellow, very smart and pleasant. On the table between us was a big block of ice. I said, 'You realise, don't you, that twenty thousand people died last winter because they were cold?'

He said, 'Well, why didn't they say something?'

I said, 'Because they are proud. That's why.'

If I do speak after a lunch for Help the Aged, it will only ever be little words. I'd like to remind people how it was the women who years ago were saying, 'Pull your gloves on, love. It's cold outside. Come on, we'll get your warm vest on.' These same women are now the ones who are *dying* of cold. And there's nobody telling them to put their gloves on, or their woolly vest on.

Scottie and I were both made life members of the Ancient Order of Foresters, who do a lot of things for charity. One year I was asked to present a little minibus we'd raised money for, to a village where there were five or six old people living at one end, and the eleven-penny dinners for senior citizens were two miles away at the other end. It's no good having a good dinner given to you if you have to walk two miles to get it. The joy when this minibus arrived! It was the best present we could have given them. One woman said to me, 'Oh, I do enjoy the little run out.'

I've helped promote Tunstall help-lines for old people to wear round their necks so they can press a button and get help, in case they have a fall . . . but we won't say any more about that or Jan will go mad. (I didn't use my own help-line when I had a fall last year, and she says she's still waiting for my explanation. The only thing I can say is, 'But I'm not old!')

I've opened old folks' homes that cost a lot to stay in, and I've opened homes that haven't cost a lot to stay. I'll never forget going with Jan to visit a home – that shall be unnamed – where you had to pay. The first room we visited was all painted white. The old lady was dressed in white. There were white flowers in a white vase. It was beautiful. And the nurse said, 'Now then, Mrs Jacobson, here's Thora come to see you.'

She said, 'Hello, Thora. How kind of you to visit me.'

Jan went round to the other side of the bed from me and said, 'Isn't it a lovely room?'

I said, 'This is my daughter, Jan.'

'Oh, hello, love. Janette Scott, aren't you?'

I said, 'It's really beautiful here.'

And this lady just looked at me and said, 'But it's not home, is it?'

And it was the way she said it. I saw Jan's face. I thought, 'Don't cry, Jan, or else I will.' But wherever I've been, that's so often the last line of the play, 'But it's not home, is it?'

Later that day we went into another part of the same home. The first room I went in to, let me tell you, was very big, with a woven carpet, and a tall glass-fronted case with beautiful glass and china in it, so you could tell there was money there. Sitting in the window seat doing embroidery was a niece, and the old lady said, 'She comes every day to see me.'

I thought, 'Yes, she will. To get the will right.'

And then Jan and I went into the next room. No pictures, just bare walls. Along the wall opposite the door we came in was a wardrobe, a coffee table and a single bed. That was the width of the room – single bed, coffee table and wardrobe. On the coffee table was a book, *The Life of Beethoven*. The woman whose room it was, I'll never forget her, had a beetroot-coloured cardigan on, her hair in a bun, and the face of an angel.

I said, 'Hello.'

I didn't know what to say to this woman in the red cardigan – because her room was so bare after the others. I said, 'Are you perfectly happy?'

And she said, 'Oh yes. Well, what more would I want?'

I said, 'I know there's a bed and a wardrobe for your clothes . . .'

'Well, I haven't many clothes.'

'I see you're reading about Beethoven.'

'I've read about them all – Mozart, Bach, Chopin . . .'

I was thinking, 'I don't know what to say.' So I said,

'Well, I hope to see you again sometime. It will be a little while. But keep your happiness with you.'

She said, 'It is so kind of you to come to see me.'

We got outside, and I was in tears. I said to the man who was running it – for money – 'We've just been to the block along there.'

He said, 'That used to belong to Dr Barnardo's. We've just bought it.'

I said, 'And is it finished, as it is now?'

'Well, yes.'

'Only I was in the first one . . .'

'Charming. A lovely room.'

'And then I was in the next one as well . . .'

'Ah, well, some of then aren't . . .'

I said, 'Don't start with that. We've just seen what some of them aren't.'

'Well, I didn't want you to go along there.'

'Why not?'

'Well, we haven't quite finished all of them.'

'Well, people shouldn't be put in them then.'

It upset me for days. Bloody days. I could see this lady's angelic face and her beetroot-coloured cardigan . . . and the book. Jan said she was sure that she was quite happy in her own way. She said, 'She's probably a minimalist and doesn't want a lot of possessions and fuss. She had her book, and she had her pride.'

I know that not everybody wants a big glass cupboard full of knick-knacks, because that's work. But oh, that bare little room did upset me. I suppose I was thinking how unhappy I would be if I had to live there myself. It was as though nobody cared if she was warm or happy. It was just a cell. It took me back to the days of the workhouse.

In Euston Road, Morecambe, the main street – main street? Ha! It's about as big as a backyard! – there used to be Pilling's, the newsagents. Mr and Mrs Pilling owned it, and then Mr Pilling died. Mrs Pilling – I don't know what she was, but I think she might have been a bit simple – went into the workhouse. Nobody knew where she'd gone, or if they did, they didn't tell us, because they didn't tell children in those days. It was quite a horrible thing, to be in the workhouse. Like Oliver Twist. The Pilling children didn't go to our school. I suppose people thought that they might get bullied by the other kids if anybody knew their mother was in the workhouse.

I went to Miss Nelson's school, Preparatory School Morecambe. 'Please Smack Me', kids from other schools used to say, because we had PSM on our school caps. We paid to go – a lot of money – one and six a week! You paid extra for music lessons and dancing classes

One day, our dancing class of twelve little girls was asked to dance in the yard of the workhouse, to entertain the people. We were all dancing along – I remember this so vividly it could have been this morning – and I saw one lady sitting in a bentwood chair watching us closely. Then I saw that it was Mrs Pilling. I didn't know whether to say, 'Hello, Mrs Pilling,' as I danced past, because she sort of turned her head away. But the next time I did. I said, 'Hello, Mrs Pilling.' She looked away with such a terrible expression on her face.

There was a councillor, Mrs Clarkeson, a big woman with a big bust, big all over, who took an interest in the schools. The following week she asked Miss Nelson if we could each write a letter to her about our visit to the workhouse, and half a crown was to be the prize for the best one.

Miss Nelson said, 'Now, we want nice handwriting, girls. And I'll give you each a sheet of foolscap, because I don't want you tearing paper out of your exercise books.' I think they expected us to write about the performance, the dancing. Most of the other girls did that. But I wrote with sympathy, didn't I? My letter was heart-rending. I wrote an Alan Bennett play about the workhouse and seeing Mrs Pilling.

'. . . *When suddenly,*' I put, because it sounded better, '*I noticed a lady sitting in a bentwood chair, and she looked so sad sitting there. When I danced round again I realised with a shock that it was somebody I knew, Mrs Pilling from the newsagents.*'

I won the half a crown.

About ten years ago I made some videotapes about old folks for Manchester Corporation. I was finding out about how people were managing on their own when they were old. I was going into people's houses and you can hear me saying, 'Should you be having that cigarette? Well, it's nothing to do with me.'

We went into this woman's kitchen, dark, and she's sitting there on her own. She's got two curl pins in her hair – I can see her now. A Thermos flask on the table. I said, 'You don't feel lonely or anything, being on your own?'

'Well, I never am on my own. Look, I've got my stick. I just bang on the fire back.' And she banged on the wall, and a minute later they came in from next door.

'What is it, love?'

'Nothing, I'm just showing Thora.'

'No,' she said to me, when they'd gone, 'what I do, Thora, I make myself a Thermos flask. So when it gets elevenses time, I pour myself a cup. If one of the neighbours wants to come in, there's two cups. If I have it early, they make me some more.'

There were some new bungalows, and one of the women living there had a daughter, a lovely Lancashire woman in her thirties, who said to me, 'Wait a minute, Miss Hird, before you go in to see my mother. She's not perhaps quite what you'd expect.'

I said, 'How do you mean? Is there anything I should know about?'

'No, but just be warned.'

So as soon as we get in the house it's, 'Eh, hello, love. Well, it is nice of you to come – will you have a cigarette?'

'Mother!' The daughter seized the cigarette, stubbed it out and took the pack.

'What are you doing?'

'Now I've told you about this.'

'Well, I don't have any when you're not here.'

'How do I know that?'

(Now I'm invisible. The film crew is invisible. The director is invisible.)

'I have told you about this. When we are not here, how do I know that you are putting it out properly in the ash-tray?'

'Well, I know when I've put a cigarette out . . .'

'You don't! It could knock off. It could be on fire. Apart from that, it's bad for you.'

'Oh well, shove off then. I want to talk to Thora.' And she turned to me saying, 'She's always interfering.'

I said, 'She's doing right.'

They were lovely, the women. I went to about four homes and a hospital. I could speak to anybody I wanted to for this tape – nothing was ever rehearsed.

So many were in hospital for their hip. I told them I'd had mine done three times. (I've had it done five times now.) I interviewed the leading man, the head doctor. He said something that made me feel sad, 'You see, Thora, a lot of people only want a bit of kindness to cure them of anything.'

I said, 'Well, being a Lancastrian, I don't know how I can believe that . . .'

He said, 'Oh well, do believe me, in a lot of homes where there's an elderly relative, the conversation goes: "Don't you think she'd be better off in hospital?" Not because there is anything the matter with them. It's more, "Get her from under my feet." '

'But it's not home, is it?'

It haunts me, that phrase. I've heard it so often. I'm trying to think of what I should say to it. You can't say, 'No, but it's your home now.' I don't know, you see. Even if you go and live with your daughter, you can't think, 'Oh, I'll get that wallpaper changed.' Once you give up your own home, life's never the same again.

My dad got £5 a week, which was a lot of money in those days. We always had a clean home. Bowl of fruit on the table with the apples polished. To this day, when I get apples I polish them. It's a habit you never get out of. Nothing on top of the piano, only at Christmas. How can you do these things when it's not your own home anymore?

A little while ago somebody rang Felix, my agent, and said, 'I hear she's living in the actors' home, Denville Hall.'

Felix said, 'Who is?'

They said, 'I'd heard Thora was.'

I'm not. They were mistaken. But I saw Doris Hare at Evelyn Laye's memorial. She does live there. She says it's marvellous. At night they get a 'half-hour' knock on the doors, like the theatre, half an hour before the bar opens before dinner. They put on shows, and agents come to see them, and a lot of them get more work now than they did before they moved there. I believe Fay

Compton was there and rumour has it she was asked to leave . . . for scandalising them! I'm not surprised – a wonderful actress, but a difficult woman. I worked with her for two years during the war. Maurice Denham is there. And Dame Diana Rigg has made her daughter promise that the moment she becomes 'a bit of a problem', she must be sent straight to Denville Hall.

And perhaps one day I will go there. I need to be able to talk to people, and the people there are all old pros. We'd have a lot to talk about. But I've still got plenty of unfinished business – and I'm going nowhere until that's done.

I think some men sometimes manage better than women do. On the tape I made for the Manchester Corporation, there was one man living in a nice house, lovely garden, detached, about five of them in a row. When I talked to him he said, 'Well, it's quite easy to look after yourself, you know. I put my long johns on at certain times of the year, and then when it gets warmer, it's just my vest, with short sleeves . . .'

I said, 'If we're going to get any more intimate, it's all going to have to be cut out of the film.'

'No,' he says, 'but I take the dog for a walk at night. Only the length of the road and back, and it can be a bit cold.'

I thought, 'Many a time you've looked at that dog, when you've to wrap up, and thought, "Blow it! Well, come on, then. Come on."'

And there was a man next door to him, who was doing his own cooking since his wife had died. He had this double boiler, a saucepan with another one on top. He had the potatoes in the bottom and the carrots in the top, and he said, 'You'll have done this, will you?'

I said, 'Well, if you wanted to save the gas it's a good idea.'

He said, 'No, well, I don't do it for that as much as I cook for tomorrow, and then I've only to warm it up.'

It's right, but it breaks your heart.

And then there were others who would say, 'Well you see, I'm not able to do much nowadays.'

And I thought, 'Yes you are, only you feel too sad to get on with it.'

So these were all the people I was thinking about, with love, as I prepared to play a ninety-year-old woman in the *Talking Heads* monologue, 'Waiting for the Telegram'. I thought of Mrs Pilling, and the old folks in Manchester, the lady in the beetroot-coloured cardigan and so many faces came back to me. Expressions and little gestures that I'd got in my mental 'library'. I knew, from talking to Alan Bennett, that my character, Violet, lived in a home. He had flatteringly told me that he'd written the part especially for me. I really looked forward to seeing the script.

I opened my copy of the script, very excited, when it arrived. Perhaps you can imagine my feelings when I read the very first line that I would have to say: 'I saw this feller's what-do-you-call-it today . . .'

My eye ran down the page. A paragraph further on I read: 'Now, Violet, was the penis erect?'

I promise you, if it wasn't Alan Bennett who had written it . . .

Talking Heads: Alan Bennett and Walter Greenwood

February 1998

12–15 February 'Waiting for the Telegram' rehearsals

February 1999

11 February Parkinson Show *5.00 p.m. car*

When I went on the *Parkinson Show* they showed an extract from Alan Bennett's *Talking Heads* monologue, 'Waiting for the Telegram'. Everyone in the studio broke down and wept. There was a man six feet two and another one six feet three in the crew, two giants. I've never seen anybody so big standing like that, with hankies. It was the bit where ninety-year-old Violet is telling the young male nurse, Francis, about the First World War, and of her young man from next door, who she loved, who was going to France the next day, and who had wanted to make love to her on his last night. And she hadn't let him. There's a pause and then she says, 'I should have let him, shouldn't I?' And nearly breaks down. I'm here to tell you, there wasn't a dry eye there, even the man on the piano . . .

I was crying myself during the rehearsals of the thing, and I said to myself, 'I'm not going to cry as much as this. No, I'm not, because it's too much. She shouldn't cry at all about it, until she gets to the very end, and maybe just a little on the "let him" perhaps as far back as that.' And as soon as I'd done that scene, rehearsing, Alan came on, knelt on the floor, put his arms round me and he said, 'Oh, bless you.'

At the very end when she said, 'There ought to be pets here, or babies', and she used her good hand to lift up the arm that's had the stroke, a bit clumsily – that upset me a bit, doing that. A lot of people remarked on that.

Oh, the numbers of people who stopped me in the street for days – weeks – afterwards to tell me about how much they had cried. They never stopped. I don't mean they never stopped crying, I mean they never stopped stopping me! One woman shook my arm the next day and said, 'I'm still crying, after last night.'

I said, 'Well, I'm not. I was only acting.'

But as a matter of fact, a lot of the times when I cry, I'm not acting. Sometimes a line of Alan's can get such a hold of me . . . I remember when we were doing the first *Talking Heads*, 'Cream Cracker under the Settee', the first rehearsal, I was very upset and kept crying as I said the lines. I apologised to Stuart Burge, the director, and I said, 'Do forgive me. I won't be like this by Friday.'

And he just looked at me and said, 'Won't you? I will!'

I had the same director for 'Waiting for the Telegram' as I had for 'Cream Cracker', Stuart Burge – he's a love. There's a part in it where she says, 'My mam – oh, she was a good 'un . . . she put some anemones in a vase . . . I love anemones . . . and put a fire in the front room', and that's when she describes the boy taking off his puttees and stripping off his khaki shirt. At the first read-through I said to Stuart, 'Stop, please. Listen. Can I make a suggestion?'

'Of course, of course.'

And I said, 'There is a tune, a song, "Goodbye, Dolly Grey" which fits with this.' It had been going round and round in my head all the way through.

There were two boys assisting Stuart and me, one on the book and one running about getting my lunch and all that sort of thing. I was glad they were there, because it's a lonely rehearsal, when you're all by yourself at Teddington. I didn't even go to the canteen. Every day after that, during rehearsals one of the lads would come in, 'Sorry. Can't get it. Can't find it.'

I said, 'Go to the BBC Music Museum . . . they've got it. I've heard it.'

They found it in the end. It was so faint, but you could hear it in the background. 'Goodbye, Dolly, I must leave you, Goodbye, Dolly Grey . . .'

I was interested in Violet's relationship with Francis, the nurse. She was ninety-four, so she wasn't in love with him, but she did love him. She'd got him a bit confused in her mind with her young man from the 1914–18 war. She'd have liked him perhaps as a son. Francis dies, and it's obviously because of AIDS, but being Alan it's never said explicitly. Violet says, 'It was a waste. He'd have made some lass a good husband.'

And it was then the girl, Devon, who wasn't a proper nurse, said, 'It wasn't lassies, it was lads with him.'

And as quick as she said it, Violet said, 'I know.' And you knew she didn't know. Because they defend, don't they? And she didn't want the girl to know that she didn't know everything about him. That's how you know she loved him, though she never said it.

It was the same thing in 'Cream Cracker', when Doris loses the baby. Alan never wrote the word 'miscarriage' – the line was, 'I wanted to call him John. But the midwife said he wasn't fit to be called anything and had we any newspaper?' What a way of telling you.

Where Alan is so brilliant is how close he gets to how people really talk. So many people remarked to me on the bit in 'Waiting for the Telegram' where Violet says, 'And this frock isn't mine. Tangerine doesn't suit me.' I think that went home to a lot of people. As we were coming out one day I said to him, 'That's very Yorkshire, that "braying on a tray with a spoon". I like that line. And Rene, the one who keeps saying, "Are you my taxi?" Have you actually seen any of these people?'

He said, 'As a matter of fact, you've picked the very one I did see. My mother was in a lovely home – if there are lovely homes. And I'm going in one lunch-time, and this woman is there, with the furs. She said to me, "Are you my taxi-driver?" as I went in. I said, "No, I'm sorry." "Well I've been ready since half past nine, and look at the time now, half past twelve."'

So Alan says to her, 'Go and sit inside and I'll go and see – he could be round the corner parked.'

So he went round the corner, no taxis, and came back to tell her there was nothing there yet, and she's telling the empty bed all this . . . 'Well, you know I was ready at half past nine. Every time I get ready, he never comes.'

'So,' he said to me, 'I didn't bother telling her it hadn't come.'

It was a fifty-minute long monologue. When I read the first few lines for the first time, the first thing I thought, honest to God, was, 'If it wasn't Alan Bennett, I wouldn't do this.' I thought, 'What's he doing? He knows the sort of thing I don't do. Oh, I wish I'd seen this months ago and told him.' And then I thought, 'No, but she's an old woman.'

Right at the start a nurse says, 'Violet, I have to ask you this. Was the penis erect?' And *I've* got to say this – because it's just me. It's a monologue of her telling us this. Now that, you see, is not an easy line to say in front of millions of people. 'Was the penis erect?'

I thought, 'Oh, I can't do this. I can't do this.' I thought about it while I was washing up and all sorts. I thought, what if I make it that it didn't matter to her that she saw it. I must make it that she'd seen little boys, she'd seen her husband, and she'd seen her own son. I must make it that she can't be bothered – it's not important. I thought of every way of doing it. I decided to mimic the voices of the different people who talk to her. So the inflection was the nurse speaking, which sort of separated it from me. I tried to put faces to all the nurses, to everyone. I put the face to Rene, 'Is my taxi there?' I could see her.

Violet has to say: 'He'd a lovely blue suit. He could have been a bank manager except he had no socks on. I said, "You can put that away."

'He said, "I've got a big detached house in Harrogate."

'I said, "That's no excuse."'

I had it in my mind that it was just the sort of daft thing you would have to put up with in a geriatric hospital. I tried to think of all the old ladies I know, or had visited in homes and hospitals, and I thought, 'They'd probably feel rather sorry for the man, or else think it was funny.' So I tried starting with a little smile: 'I saw this feller's what-do-you-call-it this morning . . .' And I thought, 'No, that doesn't sound too crude like that . . .' I just kept telling myself, 'Don't feel embarrassed. Don't feel embarrassed at rehearsal and when you get yourself ready. The beginning bit is the worst.'

And the more I did it and the more different ways I tried it out to myself – aloud – the more I felt better about it. Violet was like a lot of old people are. She wasn't easily shocked. All these things in life, Alan notices. I thought, 'Anyway, they'll probably excuse Alan Bennett if they don't excuse me.'

If you can play the truth, you can say almost anything. But two days after it came out on television, I had four plays sent to me. The first one I opened, on the second page is the four-letter word. I didn't read any more. It may have been unkind of me, but I just sent it back. The others were all the same. I am no good at those. I know that Alan Bennett doesn't write meaning things filthily. He just sits and writes because it's the truth.

I found that in 'Cracker' very much. It was ten years ago, and people still stop me in the street about it. They call it 'Biscuit under the Sofa', and all sorts. But I'm very fortunate and I mean this with my heart, that he has such a trust in me.

Little things about him I love, like when he had bought himself a Crombie overcoat. He said, 'How do you like it?' Like a little boy going to a party.

It practically reached the floor and you couldn't see his hands, only his fingertips, the arms were so long on him. I said, 'Very much. For somebody else.'

He said, 'How do you mean?'

I said, 'Well, Alan, look at it!'

'Oh! Well . . . oh, well. Well, they are a bit . . .'

I said, 'Well, of course they are.'

'I got it in a sale. It was only nine pounds.'

'I don't care if it was only nine pence – it's wrong on you. You're the great Alan Bennett.'

'Oh, I'm not. Shurrup.'

Not in the Diary

I don't want to say he's an unhappy person – I think that's too big a word. I think he's a slightly discontented person. I can't say I know him very well, except to work with him. He writes for me, and that will do. And some of the things he writes, I think, 'He thought of me.'

And he tells me he does. Sometimes I look and I think, 'That's just me.'

And he says, 'Yes, well, I can see you saying them. Like I could see you saying, "Sitting on the fender drying my hair on a Friday night, and sharing a fish and two."'

And he's right. Because we used to do exactly that, my brother Nev and I. Many is the time we've had a fish and two between us. Fish threepence, and twopenn'orth of chips were enough for two, and me drying my hair at the fire. It's very difficult, when the words are so right, when you only read them, for it not to sound right.

He told me once about coming on the bus with his Auntie Phyllis, and they were passing an old gasworks.

She said, 'Alan.'

He said, 'What?'

She said, 'You see that gasworks over there?'

He said, 'Yes. Yes?'

She said, 'It's the biggest gasworks in the north.'

He said, 'Oh, really.' But he's really not that interested, aged eleven.

She sort of puffed herself up and said, 'And I know the manager!'

★ ★ ★

I've been so lucky in my career because I have worked with two of the most brilliant writers, Alan Bennett and, a long time ago now, Walter Greenwood. Two clever men, two 'talking heads'. Walter Greenwood's comedy was about ordinary, working-class people, sitting around in pubs. He wrote several plays for me, which we put on in Blackpool and Oldham. *Love on the Dole* was his most famous play. He had an ear like Alan's for how ordinary people talk.

Walter's mother was a waitress in Manchester. He told me, 'She used to come home, did my mother, with this brown paper carrier bag full of cakes and things that had been left on all the plates. We'd only one key, so I went to bed with a string round my big toe, dangling out of the window. And my mother used to pull the string, and nearly pull my leg out of bed, to wake me up to go down and let her in.'

She used to walk to Cheadle Hulme, after she'd done a night's work, carrying this bag of crushed cakes. He said, 'Many a two o'clock in the morning I've been sitting at our kitchen table eating cake after cake. Coconut, cherry. Bits left over.'

Walter showed me the house where he lived as a child, that his father had made into a 'gentlemen's' barbershop. It was a row of houses, with a square front window, and a window above and a front door. I said to him, 'Which bedroom did you sleep in?'

He said, 'Which bedroom? There was only one. We all slept in it.'

I said to him, 'Your father didn't have much luck then, with the barbershop?'

He said, 'Well, he drank it away.'

Now there was a pub opposite, and we went in to look at where his father used to drink every night. He said, 'My mother got very disgusted with his drinking and carrying on. We had a ladder out the back. It had about ten rungs. The back street finished with a high wall, which was the wall of a reservoir. When my mother would get angry and yell at him, my father used to say – and the times I've seen him bloody do it – "That's it!" he'd say, "That's it. I'm finished. I'm going to commit suicide." This ladder was only ten treads high. The wall was another half-mile higher, and he'd get to the top tread, "Now, I'm going. You'll be sorry."

'My mother used to say, "Go on then. Commit suicide." Because she knew he was only up about two yards of this wall with this ladder.'

The pub we were in as he told me all this about his mother and father was a proper northern pub. The son of the publican was serving. There's an old fellow sitting in a corner with a bowler hat on. He says, 'Half a mild.'

And the son said, 'All right, Mr Sterndale. Half a minute.'

I was just getting the drinks in for us, so I said, 'Oh, get it for him on ours.'

So the old fellow raises his hat, 'Thank you very much. It's my birthday on Tuesday. I'll say Thora Hird bought me a drink.' Then he said, 'You know where you are, don't you?'

I said, 'Yes, I'm in a pub in Cheadle Hulme.'

He said, 'No, come here.' So I went across to him while Walter was carrying the drinks to our table. He said, 'You see that house opposite? The great Walter Greenwood was born there.'

I said, 'Well, yes, I did know that, Mr Sterndale.'

'Oh yes. Went out with my daughter for a little while. And his dad used to come in here too, you know.'

I said, 'Yes, I believe so.'

'Took a drop too much now and again, but a nice fellow.'

Walter remembered him when he started to say these things. He waited for a bit while this chap went on, but suddenly, 'Well, I *am* Walter Greenwood,' says a voice behind us. He nearly cried, did the old fellow.

Walter would tell you, if he walked in now, he'd sit down and say, 'Of course, you know, I wasn't always famous. I was eighteen before I had an overcoat.'

I used to say to him, 'Don't be telling everybody that.' God rest him, he was a great writer, and a dear, dear friend.

I know it's stupid to talk ahead; at eighty-eight, you follow. But after the BAFTA, Alan Bennett rang me from the South of France. I said, 'Well, Alan, I don't know how to put it without sounding swanky, but we got the BAFTA on your first *Talking Heads*, and now we've got it on your second. If you're ever thinking of putting me in a third, will you hurry up, because I'm eighty-eight next Friday!'

Born theatre

22 August 1998

Record Blankety Blank *5.30 p.m.*

There are people who will say to me, 'How can you still go on taking part in silly programmes like *Blankety Blank*, when you're a Dame, and especially after working with Alan Bennett?' Well, in the first place, I do it because I enjoy it. Very much. Second, working in front of an audience has been my life, and however much I get out of working with great writers like Alan, I don't want anyone to think that that makes me too snobbish to remember where my bread and butter has always come from.

For me there's nothing like performing in front of an audience. I'm still asked to do things in the legitimate theatre, but I've been saying 'no' for years. (*Legitimate* theatre – that dates me, doesn't it?) But I didn't want to be out in the evenings when Jimmy was alive, especially when we were getting older. A season at Blackpool, twice nightly, and if you're starring you've got every other line. That's a lot to learn. But I've never wanted to lose contact with the audience altogether.

I've been on *Blankety Blank* with them all – Terry Wogan, Les Dawson and now with Lily Savage. None of them fools, all of them are very clever and great fun to work with. So I hope I'll be able to go on doing that, even when nobody wants me for anything else.

I was born theatre. I grew up living next door to the Royalty Theatre, Morecambe, and from my bedroom I could hear the different plays going on below me. I've told many times how I made my first appearance on the stage when my mother carried me on instead of a prop doll, when I was a few weeks old.

When I was starting out, doing a lot of tiny parts in rep in Morecambe, I was working full-time at the Co-op, so I only used to rehearse my little bits during my lunch-hour. It was the same when I was in the billeting office at the start of the war. My lunch was from twelve until one. A bus left the battery on the promenade at twelve, and I got on just outside the Clarendon Hotel, where I worked, at two minutes past twelve. It took me down to the centre, where my mother had my sandwiches ready for me, and I rehearsed my part until quarter to one, when I caught a bus back to the Clarendon to be back at my desk for one o'clock. That's how important my parts were – I could do them in my lunch-hour.

It meant that I often didn't see the whole play we were rehearsing until we actually put it on. On one occasion I was playing the maid – I usually was – and I had to cross from one side of the stage to the other. On the opening night, as I crossed the stage, I saw a piece of crumpled paper at the back of the settee, which was in the centre of the stage. I thought to myself, 'Well, I'm the maid – I would pick that up and put it in the rubbish.' So I did.

I exited stage right and went down to the dressing-rooms. Only I heard footsteps running along behind me, and the stage manager was hissing at me, 'I suppose you know you've just walked off with the whole bloody plot?'

I said, 'What do you mean? Why?'

He said, 'It's the whole point of the plot! That bit of paper is supposed to be found in a few moments. Oh, well! We might as well not bother with Acts 2 and 3 now. We can all go home.'

I went back to the side of the stage and waited until a moment when the young couple were sitting canood-ling on the settee, then I walked on and said, 'Excuse me, Sir, I think I've left something.' As I passed I secretly dropped the bit of paper back behind them on the settee. Then I pretended to pick something up off the sideboard and walked off. I must say they looked a bit dumbfounded, because I didn't usually come on then.

Then one day George Formby came to the theatre and saw me in a play where I actually had a part. They never gave me parts. I was always the maid. Or I was a kid, with no words. Or I was a grandmother. But in this play I was acting the mother-in-law of the leading lady. Every time the girl wanted to go her own way, the mother-in-law would say, 'Oh, it's come on again! Me 'eart! See what you've done.' She was one of those.

After the performance, the owner of the theatre, Mr Moffat, came round to my dressing-room and said, 'Don't go home yet. Mr Formby wants to see you.'

I had had a paste nose on, and the paste nose was half off when he said this. I didn't know whether to push it back on or go on taking it off. But I hurried along with it half off, and George Formby, who didn't waste words, immediately started with that laugh of his: 'Hee, hee, hee! You were good! I want Ealing Studios to see you for this part, because we're making a film of it.'

The dressing-rooms were under the stage, and I can remember looking up after he'd gone, and realising that we had been standing together under the grave drop. Most stages have a 'grave drop', for when you do the gravedigger scene in *Hamlet* – 'Alas! Poor Yorick', and all that. I thought of all the times my brother Nev and I had played there, and now here I was, with a paste nose half on and half off, and this famous man had said he'd like me to do a screen test. In London. This was my Cinderella story.

Then I was on pins all the week, because I thought a man would come from Ealing the very next day to see me – which was silly. It was the Tuesday night when George Formby came in. On the Wednesday, nobody; Thursday . . . nobody. Friday night – knock on the dressing-room door, and there's a gentleman standing there in a cashmere overcoat and a thin brimmed hat, in dark brown, and a monocle. He just stood there and handed me his card, and I read: Gordon Hamilton Gaye, Casting Director, Ealing Studios.

I wasn't sure what to say, so I gabbled, 'Oh, hello. Are you on holiday in Morecambe, Mr Gaye?'

He said, 'No. I've come up from London to see you play. And it has been very well worth it. Can we go out and have some dinner?'

Now I love Morecambe, but where do you take a big cinema mogul out for dinner in the middle of winter? I thought I would have to take him to the fish and chip shop. Then I remembered that the Wellington Hotel on the promenade was what they called a 'commercial' hotel because it catered for commercial travellers. The commercial travellers would get off the train at Morecambe, and there'd be Jimmy Livingstone with a great big flat cart, handles up here, taking great trunks made of basket, full of hats and things, to the Morecambe shops like Blundell's, where I worked. He was their man for the day, for about two shillings, because they hadn't motor cars then to bring the stuff round. And they would always stay at the Wellington Hotel.

So I took Mr Gaye there, but I couldn't eat anything. I just had Horlicks.

That was the beginning of it. He said, 'We will be in touch with you for a test.'

So of course, once again, every day I'm waiting for a

letter from them. It didn't come and it didn't come, but
· eventually it came, and they enclosed a white five-pound
note for my fare to London. You have to be my age to
remember a white five-pound note. We were doing *Tony
Draws a Horse* that week, I remember, and I was Bertha
– the maid, naturally. The leading lady was called Lil
Harrold.

That night I was backstage, listening out for my cue,
and there were four other members of the cast also
behind the back-cloth, all waiting to go on at different
times. My cue was when Lil Harrold calls out, 'Bertha!'
But because I was whispering to the others and showing
them the white five-pound note, I didn't hear her. I
think it must be the only time in my life that I have
missed a cue.

I suddenly thought, 'Oh, I say, I wonder if it's nearly
time for my cue.' Just as I was putting my ear against the
door to hear where she'd got to, she flung it open . . .
and I literally fell on stage, ear first. We got a laugh that
we'd never had all week.

Towards the end of the play, I had to carry on a
silver breakfast service – things like that were always
lent to the local repertory companies by members of
the audience in those days, you could borrow anything.
And on the tray was a folded copy of the newspaper. It
was the beginning of the war, and Guy, the ASM
(assistant stage manager) was going in the Royal Navy
the next day. Normally the tray was all set and ready at
the side of the stage to carry on, with the newspaper

ready folded on the tray. But on this occasion there was no newspaper on the tray when I went to get ready to go on. There was a pile of newspapers on the side of the stage, but I said, 'Guy, where's *her* newspaper – which one is it?' Because I knew that she had a very long speech, which she hadn't learnt, and didn't need to learn, because she had it carefully pinned in the middle of her copy of the paper.

Only Guy had forgotten to bring it up. He said, 'Oh . . . well, it doesn't matter. It's Saturday. She must know the speech by now.' And he just handed me any old paper, which I took on.

All I had to say was, 'Will there be anything else, Madam?'

She's sitting at the breakfast-table in her negligee, and says 'No, thank you.' And I go off. That's all I do.

The next thing in the play is that she opens the newspaper and sees a picture of herself, and then she has this long speech. So this night, she opens the paper, expecting to find her script pinned in the middle, only it's not there. So she keeps calm. She ad-libs a bit as she casually opens the next page. No script. She opened every single page of *The Times*, and it wasn't there. She looked off-stage, where I was watching, and I thought, 'She's going to kill me.' You didn't mess with leading ladies in those days.

When we took the curtain call, I was right down at the bottom end of the cast line, and she was in the centre. As the curtain came down after the first call, she hurled the newspaper at me. Have you ever seen a newspaper that's been blown about, adhering to a railing round a garden? How it opens up and gets stuck flat? Well, this happened to me this time. When she threw it, the paper opened up and covered me from head to toe. The curtain went up again, and I bowed with everyone else, thinking it would fall off, but it didn't. It clung to me. When I stood up again, I was still completely hidden behind *The Times*.

As we were all trooping down to the dressing-rooms Lil Harrold just said, 'Oh those film people at Ealing, they don't know what they are about!'

Another time we were doing a play in rep, so I assume I'm going to be the maid, but to my joy I find out that I'm playing the grandmother, who has almost nothing to say, but is in a wheelchair. *Jane's Legacy*, that was the play. We had a lovely leading lady, Jane Mercer, a beautiful girl. She had to come on in a rather full-skirted dress, spin round and say, 'How do I look, Gran?'

One night she spun round all right – but with all the back of her dress tucked up in her knickers. She'd obviously been to the loo just before she came on. So as she spun round and said, 'How do I look, Gran?' I said, 'Come here a minute. Let me feel the material. Oh, it is nice, is this material. Oh, it is. Lovely.' And all the time I'm tugging to get this big dress out of her knickers, and she's wondering whatever is going on.

She had no idea. I didn't tell her until the end of the show, because she had another act to play and it would have put her off. At the end she said, 'Whatever were you doing?'

I said, 'Now, there's one thing that you must learn – always say to somebody "Am I all right?" after you've been to spend a penny.'

And she said, 'Oh no! What was it?'

I said, 'Well, your skirt was all tucked into your knickers.' The audience must have seen it, but I didn't tell her that. She would have been mortified.

I've never wanted to be a director myself, because I don't think I'm clever enough. I'm not just saying that for you to say, 'Oh, fancy saying that. Of course you are.' If I were directing, I'd be so busy telling them, 'Oh, you said that well.' And, 'Leave that. Keep it like that.' We would never get on with changing anything. You can be too kind – but it's better than being overcritical.

I can remember doing a play for Tennents, and a very well-known woman director – the only one in London then – was directing it. She always sat beside the footlights – I can see her shawl draped over her chair. It was a Jewish play, and I was playing the mother in it, co-starring with Frederick Valk. I had two daughters in the play; one actress was a Canadian, and very good, and the younger daughter was an attractive English actress, only seventeen, who was also extremely good. The director kept saying at rehearsal to this girl, 'No, no, no, no, no! Go off and come on again.'

She could do no right, this girl. And I saw this little face, lip trembling. Then one day this lady director says, 'I'll tell you what. I'll ask Miss Hird to have a lunch-time session with you. She'll tell you how to do it.' 'Lunch' was sandwiches that were brought round to the dressing-rooms.

I knew exactly what this girl was doing wrong – nothing. She came and sat down in my dressing-room with her sandwiches and burst into tears. She said, 'Well, I . . . you see, I don't know what to do.'

I said, 'I know what you can do.'

She said, 'Oh – what?'

I said, 'Nothing different. You're a good actress. You're only seventeen, and you're marvellous, and you're going to be even better one day. Anyone who can't see how good you were this morning isn't going to see how very good you are this afternoon. So play it just exactly the same as you are doing.'

And she did. Then the director said, 'Bravo. There you are, you see. Different as chalk and cheese! Talk to a proper actress, and you start to do it properly.'

The sad thing is, that little actress never did anything again. In my opinion, she was a great loss to the theatre.

There was a lot of kindness to my father's directing. He never got mad with anyone, even if they didn't know their words. There's no need for it, and it doesn't help anybody to give a better performance.

He was directing *The Student Prince*. There's a scene at the end of Act 2 when the men have come to tell the prince that his father is dead, and that means he's now the king. He's in love with Kathy, the barmaid in the beer-garden. The end of that scene is the old bartender putting his arm round her and saying, 'Don't cry, Kathy. He'll come back.' And her line was, 'He'll never come back.'

But the actress playing Kathy was saying it as though she was asking for 'a fish and two'. I was in this scene, playing Gretchen, the comedienne, so I heard what my father said to her. He said, 'Just try and remember, this is the man you love. You *know* he won't come back. He can't. He's the king now. The man you love has gone out of those gates, and he'll *never* come back.'

She did it again, but still as though she was saying, 'And a toasted tea cake.'

As it happened, the actor playing the student prince and the girl playing Kathy were actually having a clandestine affair. We all knew about it. Now my father would never have anything to do with scandal – he never wanted to know about it. He only wanted people to do their best. But he really was trying so hard with this girl, and nothing was getting through. So finally he said to her, 'Do pardon me mentioning this, it's no business of mine, but I think most of the company are aware that you are having a love affair with . . .' and he said the actor's name that was playing the student prince. And he said, 'Please try to imagine how you would feel if you knew you were never going to see him again.'

She was crying as she said, 'How dare you!'

He just said, 'Now say your line.'

Still crying she said, 'He'll never come back!'

He said, 'That'll do. Keep it like that.'

He had forced her to act from real feeling, you see. He was ahead of his time, my father. Dick Sharples, who wrote the television series *In Loving Memory* and *Hallelujah!*, always said, 'I'd have loved to have met your Dad.'

As I began this chapter by saying, I was born theatre, and acting is my life. Doing lots of different things, being somebody else for a few hours, living somewhere else, this is why I am never bored. I love it. Sir John Gielgud was being interviewed on television the other day – aged ninety-five – and he said that the thing he missed most was the camaraderie of the rehearsal room. So many actors would agree with that. But to do a play in a theatre in the West End now would be very, very difficult for me, except perhaps for a one-night performance gala evening.

For one thing, I'd now have to say, 'She doesn't sit down and then get up, does she? Because I can't do that. She doesn't ever walk across the stage, does she? Because I can't do that.'

They'd say, 'Well, what can you do?'

'I'll tell you what I can do. I can sit in a chair and say the Lord's Prayer.'

And I can – because I've such a lot to thank him for.

Family, friends and the extended tea room

July 1998

11 July Lunch Felix
12 July Lunch Sandy
14 July Rob coffee
    2.00 p.m. Teddington (Alan Bell)
16 July 10.30 a.m. Shepperton Studios
    4.00 p.m. Brian tea
18 July Russell Hotel
19 July 4 p.m. Nicky
20–24 July Victoria Wood TV Centre
26 July Radio Times *interview*
27–28 July Pinewood Studios
29 July Daily Express *lunch*
30 July Ready Steady Cook

People say to me, 'Why don't you live next door to your daughter in your beautiful cottage in the country?'

They say it to Jan, too, I know – asking her why doesn't she suggest that I go and live there. But just look at a few of the dates in my diary – one day lunch with Felix, my agent; the next day lunch with Sandy, my great friend from Help the Aged; the next day Rob for coffee, that's Rev. Rob Marshall, Vicar of St Augustine's, South Kensington, and a great friend of mine.

All these things couldn't happen in the country. How could they? And I love it all, you see. Friends calling round for tea or coffee. There were five people sitting on the sofa the other morning. Charity lunches. Pinewood and the BBC Television Centre for rehearsals. *Ready Steady Cook*. It's my life. I'd be lonely if the telephone wasn't forever going with someone saying, 'Can I come round at coffee time?' Of course my favourite visitor of all is my daughter. The two things in life that give me the greatest pride and pleasure in the world are my daughter and my work. Without those two things I think I would be lost. Well, I don't think – I know.

A lot of people come to interview me for a programme or a magazine, or to take my photograph for an appeal. I always say, 'Well, if you come about nine, there'll be coffee.' And a lot of them bring me flowers when they come – it's very nice. With so many friends like Roger Royle from *Sunday Half Hour*, acting pals like Brian Rawnsley, Kathy Staff, Dora Bryan, and the director Alan Bell, who all drop in regularly for a tea or a coffee – I sometimes don't know whether I've got an extended family, or an extended tea room.

I don't do lunches. I take people out to lunch. It's so easy with a lovely little Greek restaurant at the top of the mews. Scottie used to do the lunches. He was a superb cook, his sauces were a legend, and we both loved to give lunch and dinner parties. Our dining-room table has seated so many friends and heard so much laughter over the years, but I hardly ever sit at it for my meals now. That's a little bit of life that's passed.

There's no need to feel sorry for me. I have a lovely laughing photograph of Scottie placed where I can see it from my chair. That face is exactly like him. They say you never get over it, but I said to God, 'Will you help me with this.' And he has. I feel that Scottie is so near me. I don't mean I see him or anything, but he really does seem to be here with me. When I come into the room I look across at his photograph and he laughs at me.

Funnily enough, the times that I miss him most are not when I'm feeling a bit low – because he's always with me then. It's more when something wonderful has happened, like winning the BAFTA. It's not the same, having a success, when somebody you love isn't there to say, 'Isn't it nice?' Don't think I'm not grateful. There is not a more grateful person in the world than me.

When I won the BAFTA, my grandchildren Daisy and James sent me a little photograph case, with their photographs in – that talked! I keep it in my handbag. You press a button and you can hear their voices saying,

Daisy: Congratulations on the BAFTA, Ganny!
James: Congratulations, Ganny, we're proud of you!

Daisy: And we love you very much.
James: Now don't touch that red button!
Daisy: Egg custard!

Egg custard – that's Daisy's and my secret sign. We always have to say it before we say goodbye. The red button is because the first one they sent me, I pressed the red button, which is for recording, instead of the green button, which is for listening, so I never heard their message the first time. Jan took it back to America and they did it again for me.

I don't see so much of them now, because Daisy and James both live and work in Los Angeles. They keep in touch with their mother with letters and faxes and telephone calls, and Jan always passes on their news and their love to me, but they are both making their own way in the world now, so they don't come back to England very often. Daisy sends faxes to her mother four times a week. They are all very close, but you can't be as close as you'd like to be when it's only through letters. I've got a little blouse with daisies on, so I'll send that to Daisy this week. Jan says, 'You're silly to keep buying her things. You don't know what her taste is.'

I said, 'I know. That's true.'

I did get her a sweater with a line of daisies across, in navy blue, and she loved that. But you're not lucky every time. At least it shows her I love her and am thinking about her.

They have grown up in the world of show business,

with Janette Scott for their mother, Mel Tormé their father and me their 'Ganny'. At the moment Daisy is in a group that does voice-overs for television, films and cartoons. To explain what she does, think of an American television show like *ER*. As that hunky, gorgeous doctor, whatever his name is, is walking through the main reception area at the hospital, you might hear a nasal voice over the tannoy going, 'Will Dr Rhubarb please come to the Emergency Room immediately . . .' That will be Daisy. If there's a scene of a street shoot-out, or a crash, the voices shouting, 'Oh good gad! Don't move!' or 'You'll be all right, darling . . .' or 'Who *was* that?' will be Daisy and her group. They do all the background noises and voices. It's a small beginning, but it pays the rent.

She has another job, to which she gives as many hours as she can. It's a Web site sports fan club, where she is the liaison between sports stars and their fans. She finds out what news they want to put out on the Web site, and then she writes it up for them, which she can do in her own time from her home computer. She's profoundly knowledgable on all sports, and loves it.

James is in his last year at University College of Los Angeles, reading English and history – graduating purely for his mother. But it's something that can never be taken away from him once he's done it. He can't chuck it away.

He is undoubtedly going to spend a couple of years as a performer, although Jan thinks that his real strength is as a writer. His lyrics for songs are wonderful – well, we think so. He already has a couple of recording contracts being dangled in front of him. He is also an excellent actor. I saw him in a play at school, and he was so good I couldn't find the words to tell him properly. I had to write him a letter later. It will depend what chances come, which road he will eventually take.

The sadness is that they don't get over here very often. They both adore England. I think James would live in England given the chance, but the hard fact is in this modern world you have to live where the opportunities are, and at this point in both their young lives there are more opportunities for budding show-business careers in California than in rural Sussex.

Talking about families, something has happened recently that has really delighted me. I received a letter from a Mrs Vernon, who lives in Jersey. Mrs Vernon, who I have never met, must be a relation, because she has sent me part of my father's family tree which I'd never seen before, with the names and dates of my great-grandparents and my grandfather, the pirate, and all his brothers and sisters, and there is something about it that is very interesting.

I see that my great-grandfather, William Hird, who was born in 1811 and died in 1885, came from Fifeshire, Scotland. The Kingdom of Fife. Now that was always my father's boast; he'd say, 'We're a Fifeshire family.' But until now I never knew why he said that. Scottie had an auntie in Forfar, but I never knew that I had family roots up there too.

Jimmy's Auntie Emma in Forfar only put her teeth in to go and draw her pension, but if she looked out of the window of her butt'n'ben in the Highlands she could see Glamis. She was only about four foot six, a tiny little Scots, lovely thing. She wore one of these bonnets with the frill on to hold strawberries.

Her swank of life – of *life* – was seeing the Queen Mother. 'I took one look at her and I smiled, and do you know, she smiled back?' This was when the Queen Mother was a young girl at Glamis. 'Oh, she was very pretty. And I just looked at her and gave her a wee smile, and she looked at me and she smiled back.'

My dad never said, 'We're a Lancashire family.' And now I know a second reason for that, thanks to Mrs Vernon sending me the family tree. My great-grand-mother, Betty Redman, who married William Hird, was born in 1819 at Hebden Bridge. J.B. Priestley, that gravelly voice of wartime radio, used to call Hebden Bridge 'the region of mountaineering trams'. When I was a child you could go by tram all the way across the hills to Leeds – and that gives the game away. Hebden Bridge is the furthest point west you could go in the West Riding of . . . Yorkshire. *Yorkshire!*

Great-grandfather was one of fifteen brothers. They all had auburn hair except one, who was dark – so that's where my hair comes from, and my granddaughter Daisy's. So these two, my great-grandparents, William and Betty Hird, settled in Yorkshire after they were married and nearly all their children, including my own grandfather, William Hird, who grew up to be the red-haired buccaneer, were born there. So my grandfather's family were half Scottish and half Yorkshire. He was not from Lancashire at all.

My father was born in Todmorden, which is half in Lancashire and half in Yorkshire, and once he had married my mother, who was true Lancashire, they lived in Morecambe. I still feel very Lancashire, but I'm sincerely glad to know that there's a bit of Scot, like my beloved Scottie, and a bit of Yorkshire in me somewhere as well. I never held with all that rivalry between Yorkshire and Lancashire.

27 May 1999

The night before my eighty-eighth birthday

I've some peculiar friends, but none more peculiar – or funny – than Barry Cryer. On the night before my birthday Michael King, of the King Brothers (a group best remembered for their hit version of 'Wake up, Little Susie' in the late fifties), took Jan and me to the King's Head in Islington. That's the little London theatre that is also a pub where you can eat your dinner and watch the show. They were doing *A Saint She Ain't*, with music composed by Michael's brother, Denis King, and produced by Ned Sherrin. It has since transferred to the Apollo, in the West End, with some of the best reviews you've ever seen in your life. It was a very funny show, about people pretending to be stars of the forties, like the Andrews Sisters, Betty Grable and Ethel Merman, performing a rather obscure Molière comedy about mistaken identity. Barry Cryer was playing W.C. Fields.

The King Brothers were three brothers – Michael, Denis and Tony – and they were all great friends when Jan was a teenager. But the real secret of why we were there is Michael. Michael was the special sweetheart. Then, in the way these things happen, they lost touch until last year when, out of the blue, Michael wrote to tell Jan that his mother, who had always been very fond of Jan, had died. Of course Jan wrote back to say how sad she was, and then she put, 'This is silly. Can we not meet up again?' So that's why we were all at the King's Head together that evening.

It was odd to see him again, Michael, a man in his sixties, because to me he will always be a teenager holding hands with my teenage daughter. We also sat with Peter O'Toole that night. He had come straight from rehearsal for the revival of *Jeffrey Barnard is Unwell*, also being produced by Ned Sherrin. As soon as he walked in he came over and said 'Hello' to me.

I hardly know him, but I'm well brought up. I said, 'Hello.'

Someone offered him a chair, and he said, 'No, I want to sit at her feet.'

He was very flattering and charming, and he must have told me three or four times that night how much I reminded him of his own mother.

After the show, we stayed sitting at our table, and Barry Cryer, who was marvellous as W.C. Fields, joined us for cake and champagne to celebrate my birthday. Now there were two women at the next table with what looked like a sherry each. And they were sitting as though they were playing statues, looking at us. I turned and said to Barry, 'Would you mind going away. You've been nothing but a damned nuisance all night, and it's gone on for far too long.'

He stood there with his hat in his hands, and he hung his head and said, 'Well, it's just my admiration for you . . .'

I said, 'Never mind about that. You've been a damned nuisance for ten years . . .'

Very silly, I know. But even at our great age, we do so enjoy acting whenever there's an audience – even when it's only two ladies. And it *was* my birthday!

So with my life as busy as it has ever been, and with so many people calling round for a coffee, I'll be staying on in the mews for a while yet, running my extended tea room. So you needn't be telling Jan off for not having me to live with her. I'm just not cut out for country life. Scottie was. He loved the cottage and the garden and if he'd been the one left, he'd have moved down there like a shot. As it is, I'm happier in the home I've lived in all my married life, surrounded by my friends and neighbours, and with my photographs of his dear face, and all my memories.

I've always got the Lord, if I'm ever lonely.

How's biz?

January 1998

19 January Call my Bluff *11.30 a.m. car*

It gives me great pleasure whenever I'm invited to take part in the television panel game *Call my Bluff*, which goes out in the mornings most weekdays. I suppose I must have been doing it once or twice a year from the beginning. I have known Alan Coren for ever, and more recently I've got to know and love Sandy Toksvig, a marvellously clever girl. They are the two team captains nowadays, if you've never seen the game. It used to be Frank Muir and lovely old Arthur Marshall, who used to laugh silently with shaking shoulders. And before that one of the team captains was Patrick Campbell, the aristocratic Irishman with the stammer, and Robert Robinson was the chairman. Do you remember them all? Oh, I do.

Anyway, how you play it is that one team – there are three of you in each team – is given an obscure word out of the dictionary, and two of you read out a completely false definition and one of you reads out the true definition. Then the three members of the opposite team have to decide which one of you is telling the truth. All the definitions are intended to confuse your opponents, and sometimes I like to tell a story of my own to illustrate a word. I think it was the last time I was on that I told this story – don't ask me to remember the word I was defining. It was probably *flubbliduck* or something equally daft. But this was the story I told:

During the war it was an accepted thing that if you were in a West End theatre, you would give a night or two, after your own show, to do a turn at the Nuffield Centre, where our lads gathered before they went off overseas.

One night after I left the Nuffield Centre, having done my little act, I went to Oxford Circus tube. During the war, down in the underground would be people asleep, using it as an air-raid shelter. Babies, mothers, grand-mothers, family dog, all wrapped up and sleeping on the platforms. But there was some law that meant that half the platform had to be kept for people using the trains. So on my platform there were all these people fast asleep at one end, and at the other end was nothing and nobody, except for a weighing-machine, painted red.

Now on this particular night, I was wearing a red coat, and my hair in those days was a shade or two redder than it is now. I was standing there, all in red, next to the red weighing-machine, waiting for my train, when a GI came down onto the platform. With a big cigar and a slight sway on, because he was a bit tipsy. Please don't think I've any disrespect for the American soldiers, but they did rather think that we were there for their convenience, and this one was definitely the worse for wear.

I've always been afraid of drunks. I don't know why. My mother used to say, 'All you've got to do is push them.' But nevertheless, I could never rid myself of this fear.

As he came past me the GI said, 'Hya, Red.'

I didn't know whether he meant my coat, my hair or the weighing-machine. So I didn't answer. He said, 'Hey! I'm talking to you.'

I said, 'I'm not talking to you.'

Which was silly, because saying that, I was talking to him. Anyhow, unless you live in London you may not be acquainted with the noise of a tube train from out of a tunnel, you hear a 'boom boom boom' rumbling sound from a long way off. I heard this sound now, and I was most grateful. The train came in and the doors slid open while he was standing there saying to me, 'Well, don't let's talk. What do you charge?'

Now, I'm not a smart Alec as a rule, who can think of a very comic remark to say back to people. Some people are very good at it, but I'm not. However, on this occasion I think I did come up with something rather brilliant. I backed away from him into the train, and with perfect theatre timing I said, 'Well, what do your mother and sister charge?' just as the doors slid closed in front of his face and the train pulled away with me safely on it. I could see his face, as he stood there, nearly crying.

And that, ladies and gentlemen, is the meaning of 'flubbliduck' – a smart answer perfectly timed.

In the old days, just after the war and in the fifties, in the Bayswater Road there would be a girl every few yards. And cars pulled up. There was a madam who used to wear a man's black overcoat and men's shoes, and a turban in black with a *kohinoor* on the front, the stone was really that big, and a man's umbrella. She was going about selling her business wares – which all took place in Lancaster Mews, where she had about three houses I believe. You'd see her every night, this woman. Apparently her children went to the best schools in England.

It's all been stopped now. 'The streets have been cleared.' At the top of the mews that I live in there's a very nice pub with a rail round it. In those early days there was always the same woman standing at the railings of this pub. She was like a miniature Mae West. Black velvet ribbon round her throat, with a diamond as big as the Ritz. She was there most nights.

I would get out of the taxi as I came back from the theatre, at the top, so the taxi didn't need to come down the mews and turn round. She'd always say to me, 'Goodnight, dear. How's biz?'

I would say, 'Oh, very good tonight, thank you.'

We were always very polite. Well, one night I got out at the top as usual, but I was with Scottie, and he got out of the cab first so she didn't see me. She looked at him and called out ever so perkily, 'Are you satisfied, dear?'

I put my face round and said, 'He'd better be!'

She wasn't in the least embarrassed by this. She just said, 'Oh, goodnight, dear. How's biz?'

Last of the Summer Wine?

October 1998

13 October Photograph Observer. Cancelled
14 October Pinewood filming day. Cancelled
15 October chiropodist. Cancelled
Gala dinner, Celebrities Guild of Great Britain, Dorchester Hotel. Cancelled
25 October Lady Ratling's Ball with Roger Royle.
Cancelled

It looks awful, doesn't it? A diary full of cancellations. To start off with, about a week earlier, I was sitting on the stool in the back kitchen topping and tailing and shredding French beans for a spot of lunch. You know how you have to tear the long stringy bits off the sides? I'd got a little pile done and I thought, 'That's enough, just for one.'

I got off the stool, started to move away and I don't know how but I got one foot caught over the other and I fell. Thump. I lay there for a little tick having a meeting with myself, thinking, 'Now wait a minute. If I get hold of the little door under the sink.' But it just came open, and didn't help me. I got hold of the handle on the stove door – and that came open. Everything I tried to get a hold of swung open downwards or sideways and I was still on the floor. I've got a Tunstall life-line that you are supposed to press when you have a fall and somebody comes, but – and this makes Jan so mad – I didn't like to bother them.

Eventually I managed to get up, and I am delighted to say I didn't feel any the worse. Just a bit thumped, as you do.

Well, about a week later I was going out to a charity dinner, and Alan Bell was escorting me because I hadn't a Jimmy. I was dressed and ready. I don't keep people waiting. I've a lot of faults, but not that one. The car drew up outside, Alan came in, and I was absolutely ready to go.

He said, 'How do you feel?'

I said, 'Not so bad,' and then I heard somebody scream.

I remember thinking, 'Is that someone in the mews?' And then I don't remember another thing. I don't remember my neighbour Jane running in. I don't remember the ambulance arriving down the mews with its siren going. Jane and Alan both came to the hospital with me. Jane stayed there until Jan could get up from the country. So I've been told. I don't remember a thing.

Because it was me that had screamed. Isn't it funny, this? It sounds so dramatic that it sounds ridiculous, but it's true.

To this day, I can't tell you exactly what it was. I thought they said I'd broken two arteries in my leg, but

Jan says that isn't right. She says that I must have somehow dislocated my artificial hip-joint. I know arteries come into it somewhere, because there was some problem with the flow of blood to my foot. I couldn't feel my right foot. They didn't tell me, but they told Jan they might have to amputate. Thank goodness it never came to that. Whatever happened that night, the pain made me unconscious. I was in hospital for about three weeks.

As soon as I arrived, they took away all my rings and jewellery to put it in the hospital safe. But I wouldn't let them take my cross off. I practically fought them for it. Scottie bought it for me in a little shop in Holland. It was one of the last things he ever gave me.

Once Jan arrived, she wouldn't leave me, so they put a chair for her next to my bed, and we both went to sleep. For the next two weeks she did everything for me, and stayed with me every night. Then they moved me into a different ward, and they wouldn't allow Jan to stay beside me any longer. The first morning after she had gone, I woke up to find that somebody had stolen my cross.

When I was leaving the hospital, a few weeks later, one of the senior doctors said to me, 'Are you going straight back to work in television?'

I said, 'No, I've to write a book first.'

He said, 'What about?'

I said, 'This hospital.'

He looked rather pleased, and said, 'Oh! What will you call it?'

I said, '*Just a Minute.*'

Anything you asked for, that was the answer you got, 'Just a minute . . .' and then you'd have to wait and wait. There was an old lady in the bed opposite me with a very weak, soft voice who kept calling, 'Nurse. Nurse.'

I said to her, 'Have you got a button?'

But she just went on, 'Nurse, nurse, nurse . . .'

So I thought, 'Well, if I press mine, a nurse will come.'

So I pressed mine. A nurse came over and switched it off. She said, 'Will you stop disrupting the running of this hospital.'

Now I don't expect to be treated any differently from anybody else, but I'd never rung my bell before. I said, 'I was ringing the bell for that lady over there. I think she wants a bedpan.' By the time they got to her it was too late, of course, so they had to change all the bedclothes and everything, and I'm sorry if it sounds unchristian, but I thought, 'Good.'

'Patient' was the right word for what you had to be. I know they are all very overworked and it must be very stressful work, but do they need to be so rude? I know I'm not the only one who has felt this.

I was there for some time. I don't know how long exactly, about three weeks, but I was worried because I was meant to be finishing the filming for *Last of the Summer Wine*. That cancelled filming day on 14 October in my diary was meant to be for finishing off a couple of scenes.

I can't remember all the details about what did happen, so Jan will tell you this next part of the story.

Jan's story

With Mother in hospital, it looked as though she would be unable to complete her part of the work on *Last of the Summer Wine*. They had almost completed ten episodes, and just needed to finish some of the scenes at the ladies' coffee mornings. The set of Edie's living-room was the last to be put up in Pinewood Studios, where they had rented a floor for three weeks. Mother had a few lines to say that were absolutely essential to make sense of these final scenes. They needed her not just to say the lines, which could have been recorded from the hospital bed, but to be there, on the set with the others. They needed to see her facial expression.

Apart from the massive expense of renting a film floor at Pinewood Studios, they would soon have to dismantle the set because something like a James Bond film was coming in the following week. So even if they could have afforded another week, which they couldn't, it was impossible for them to keep the set together once the three weeks was up.

Alan Bell, the director, was of course very anxious for Mother, but said that if there was some way of arranging it, all she would be asked to do was to sit at her table on the set, and speak her remaining few lines. Mother was more than willing to do it, as she had been worrying about not being there. I discussed with Alan the fact that she was under heavy medication for the pain and I didn't think that she would be able to remember any long speeches. We hatched the plan of him saying her lines, one at a time, and her acting them straight back at him.

I went to the doctors and asked them whether – in four or five days' time, if she was well taken care of, with an ambulance taking her there and back and no walking involved – it would be possible for her to go to Pinewood to complete this filming. Well, of course, doctors have no idea about 'the show must go on'. They didn't begin to understand about the number of people involved, the massive amounts of money, and the general urgency and importance of the thing.

However, they were eventually persuaded that perhaps it would be all right, but the rules were – and I had to swear to keep them by all that was precious to me – that Alan Bell and the BBC production team of *Last of the Summer Wine* would arrange for:

a) a private ambulance to come and pick my mother up;
b) a private doctor in constant attendance;
c) a private nurse in constant attendance;
d) The ambulance would come at eleven o'clock in the morning, after the doctors' morning round, take her

to Pinewood, and deliver her right onto the set, where she would be moved in a wheelchair. She would say her lines, be put back in the ambulance and arrive back at St Mary's by five o'clock in the afternoon, ready for the doctors' afternoon round. Then they would see that she was still alive and kicking and no harm had come to her.

So that was all agreed. Alan and I arranged for her hairdresser to come to the hospital in the morning, along with the make-up lady and dresser with her costume, so that her hair would be done, and she could be dressed and made up, all on her bed at St Mary's, Paddington. So the party for the ambulance to Pinewood would be a hairdresser, a make-up artist, a wardrobe mistress, a private doctor, a private nurse, Mother and me.

On the morning that she was due to do it, all this having been arranged, the hospital doctors came to her bed on their morning round, where they looked at her and muttered and tut-tutted a bit and then they said, 'Mmm, no. We think that she's not well enough. We don't think we can let her out of the hospital today.'

I, who at this point had taken up house in the chair next to my mother's bed, and was sleeping there at night, leapt from my chair and grabbed hold of the lapels of the senior doctor and practically screamed in frustration, 'But you don't understand! There are several hundred people involved in this! She has *got* to do it!'

So finally, still not at all willing for her to go, and not

understanding in the least why it was so important, the doctors had me sign various forms where they completely washed their hands of all responsibility for my mother's wellbeing and put it all on me.

Then they filed out of the ward, each of them looking at me as though they thought I was going to murder my own mother. And secretly I began to feel a little bit like that myself – supposing they were right? This was the awful thing. And yet, in my heart of hearts I knew that not finishing the series was worrying Mother dreadfully, because she felt that she was letting so many people down. I knew it was preying on her mind.

At that point there was still a great question-mark over whether or not her foot should be amputated because her clogged arteries were preventing the blood from reaching it. This was a real possibility. I thought that if that happened, if she never worked again, she would never forgive herself for not having finished the last job. It was psychologically of vital importance.

So, the hairdresser arrives, and the make-up artist arrives and the wardrobe mistress arrives. Mother is all prepared, lying on the bed dressed up and completely ready to go at eleven o'clock, waiting for the private ambulance plus doctor plus nurse to arrive . . . And nothing happens. No ambulance.

I am running up and down the stairs of St Mary's, looking up and down the street, waiting and waiting. Running back and forth. Telephoning Alan Bell to see if he knows why it hasn't come. No, they are all there waiting for us to arrive. Twelve o'clock came. One o'clock. No sign of the ambulance. By this time I was afraid that even if we got her to Pinewood Studios, she wouldn't be back for five o'clock, and St Mary's would refuse to let her back in . . . or they would tell me that I had done her irreparable damage and it was *All My Fault*.

However, the ambulance finally arrived with their tale of woe just after one o'clock. Apparently, any private ambulance must, by law, stop and offer assistance if there is an accident. On their way to the hospital there had been a major accident directly in front of them, involving a car, a motorbike and a lady on a push-bike. They had had to stop and take all these people to the nearest casualty department.

So, of course, we all felt, 'Well, thank God they were there to help these people.' But another part of my mind was in a complete panic, saying, 'Come on, come on! Drive like crazy!'

So like Toad in *The Wind in the Willows*, the ambulance driver rang his bell and beeped his horn and hurtled along the motorway to Iver Heath in Buckinghamshire, to Pinewood Studios . . . with Mother on the bed, the doctor, the nurse, the hairdresser, the make-up girl, the wardrobe mistress, and me all jammed together beside her.

The extraordinary thing was to see my mother – who had entered the ambulance as a patient of St Mary's Hospital, Paddington, very ill, very weak and in great pain – metamorphosing into Thora Hird, actress, as we passed through the studio gates at Pinewood. Literally as we drove through the big mock-Tudor entrance gates, with the Rank sign of the man banging his gong, her eyes sharpened and brightened. She knew where she was, she knew what she was there for, this was her world, she was in charge of herself and of everything going on around her.

A pathway was made for her as the wheelchair processed with her through the film unit right up to where the camera was set up and everyone was waiting. She was lifted from the wheelchair to a chair on the set. She did her work, giving a brilliant and comic performance. Sarah Thomas, who plays her daughter in *Last of the Summer Wine*, was quite magnificent. She was completely unselfish and generous, and helped my mother enormously to give the performance she wanted to give. I was incredibly grateful to her for that.

The whole thing can't have taken more than forty-five minutes – an hour at the most. Alan Bell said, 'That's it. Thank you, everyone.' Then the entire unit rose to their feet and gave Mother a standing ovation.

Mother was lifted back into her wheelchair, put back in the ambulance, and we hurtled back to St Mary's, Paddington. There was no harm done, but in a strange way I am quite certain that Mother would have died happy as long as she had finished her work. To leave it incomplete would have been unthinkable to her.

Worrying about it had been making her unhappy. Ten days after this escapade, she was well enough to go home.

Jan can remember and tell you so much better than I can. The only thing I do remember is going back to the hospital from the studio in the ambulance and thinking, 'I wish they were taking me home.'

But eventually I did get home. At first I needed a full-time nurse. One from eight in the morning until eight at night, and then another one came from eight at night until eight the next morning. It cost me thousands. All I can say is, I'm grateful I had it. When you need day and night care, you can't expect even the most loving daughter, as Jan is, to stay and do everything for me all the time. By the time I came out of hospital, in any case, Jan was totally exhausted, because she'd been with me and done everything for me almost the entire time I was there.

My difficulty now is – I can't get up. That's why I can't have anything in my part written where I have to stand up. I can't do it. I told Alan Bell, who visited me nearly every day when I was in hospital. When I came home he came round and I said, 'Alan, I never thought I'd have to say this, but I don't think I can do the next lot.'

'I'm not listening.'

I said, 'But look at me! I don't think I can do them.'

'I'm not listening.'

Last of the Summer Wine?

I said, 'Well, what will you do?'
He said, 'You'll be in them, sitting down all the time.'
I said, 'Oh, that *will* be good. Never getting up.'

That was in 1998. I'm now looking in my diary for 1999:

July Filming Last of the Summer Wine, *Pinewood*
September Filming Last of the Summer Wine, *Holmfirth*
October Filming days, Pinewood

And there's to be another ten this year. I was so pleased for Alan, and for all of us, when *Last of the Summer Wine* got the Royal Television Society Best Comedy Series Award in 1999. About bloody time, if you ask me. Everyone loves it – the audiences do. It's been going for ever, but it's never been given anything before. The BBC act as though they are ashamed of it, the amount of attention they pay it.

So I was back in harness again last year. Only 1999, oh dear, that was the year that dear Bill Owen died, God rest him. I have known him all my life, nearly, since the thirties, when we both started out as young actors at Ealing Studios. Bill would come into rehearsal in a jaunty little check hat, sling bag over his shoulder, come up to me and kiss me, 'Mornin', darlin'.'

He was a little wonder as Compo. We'd only done five of the ten programmes in the 1999 series, and were still in the middle of filming the fifth one when Bill was taken gravely ill, and died a few weeks later. One day when we were filming, I had a line to him – the three men were all going to France – my line was, 'But you *are* going abroad. You're going to France. Now cheer up.'

What I had planned to do was the old gag of giving him a good old slap across the face when I said, 'Now cheer up!' But he looked so poorly, I just said the line, 'Now cheer up,' and gave him a little look. I couldn't have slapped him across the face, even to give him a pretend, stage slap. It was the last thing I did with him.

We all thought that would be the end of it, with Compo gone. But we were contracted to do a series of ten programmes, and Alan Bell said we must carry on. And we did. Bill Owen's son, Tom Simmonite, has come into it, as Compo's son. He's the image of him. The image. You could do a close-up of him and think it was Bill himself. He's very funny, and very good.

Kathy Staff, as Compo's beloved Nora Batty, had the last line at the ladies' coffee morning – in the café – that said it all. She had to get the timing just right, which she did. If you don't hold the pause long enough, it sounds like nothing – if you make the pause too long, the audience thinks, 'Hello, here's a sad line coming' and it doesn't work. I've forgotten exactly what her line was, but it was like:

Well, he was nothing but bother . . . (*pause*)
but it's going to be very quiet where I live now.

Holmfirth went into full mourning for him. One day the whole cast and the crew went to the churchyard where Bill is buried. From the very start of coming to film the very first series he had said, 'I want to be buried here', and bought himself a plot.

There's a little hill at the back of the church, smooth green grass, and one grave there. Hosts of flowers. Somebody had left a pair of child's wellingtons on top of the grave.

One of the crew said, 'It doesn't look right, somehow.'

And Bill's dresser, a dear, dear man, turned the tops down of the wellingtons and said, 'It looks right now.'

Two laughs for one

25 March – 5 April 1998

Lost for Words *Rehearsals, Leeds*

We had two weeks to rehearse Derek Longden's television film about his mother, *Lost for Words*. Alan Bell
was directing, and that fine actor Peter Postlethwaite
played the son. He even looked a bit like Derek, so he
was right for the part. He was surprised when I suggested
to Alan a couple of times during rehearsals that a line or
a bit of business written for me might be better coming
from Peter.

He said, 'Why would you want to do that?'

I said, 'Because it's best for the play. That's why.'

Acting is about everybody working together. That's
what my father taught me. It's no good unless you're
all good. Years ago, when I was playing Blackpool,
which I did a time or two, Harold Boyes was business
manager for George and Alfred Black at the Grand.
At rehearsal one day I said to the director, 'I think
that line of mine would be better coming from the
daughter.'

Harold, who was watching, said to me afterwards, 'I
don't know what's the matter with you – giving away a

good laugh like that. That's a powerful line.'

I said, 'If *I* say it, I'm giving away a good laugh. If she says the line – laugh – and then my facial expression when I hear what she says – another laugh. That's two laughs instead of one.'

He said, 'Well, that doesn't always happen.'

I said, 'It never misses with me. And there's another line of mine that's better for the son to say. He'll say it . . . they'll all laugh. And then I'll clout him. Two laughs.'

I'm not a goody-goody in the theatre, but it's no good being arrogant, 'Well, I know how to do this so I should have all the best lines.' It's teamwork. A play is only as good as you all are. My father used to say, 'Never begrudge another cast member anything.'

I remember one boy coming to us in Blackpool from being in *Chips with Everything*. Freddie Frinton and I had been doing *Meet the Wife* on television and *My Perfect Husband* was especially written by my brother, Nev, for the same characters. This young lad came in it to be our son, and he played the guitar, because it was that period when you always had to have that. Joe Gladwyn was playing Granddad – beautifully. He was only on in Act 3, but he got a laugh with every line. It was only a small part, but he was very, very good. He had to be sitting down at stage right for his scene as Granddad. The lad who was playing my son kept standing in front of him, masking him from the audience. Joe came to me one morning and said, 'Please don't think I want to bring a complaint against him, but it's the only scene I've got.'

I came down to the front and watched them. I thought, 'You little sod. Just because he's getting a laugh a line.'

So I sent for the lad, between the first and second house – we were always on twice nightly at Blackpool. I didn't give him a note – I nearly gave him a thick ear. I said, 'Joe's only got that one scene in the play, and he's very good.'

He said, 'Yes, I know.'

I said, 'Well, you don't know. You don't know anything. You're ruining it for him. From now on, you stay where you were put, over by the table. And you can stop standing in front of Joe, just because he's getting a lot of laughs. Being in *Chips with Everything* doesn't make you a great actor.'

He said, 'Oh well, OK. My mother and father are in tonight.'

I said, 'Well good. You stay back, or else I'm going to walk on and say to you, "Get out. Your grandfather's fed up of you." And you'll have to go off and miss your best scene.'

He never stood in front of Joe again.

My father taught me so much about the business. It was like a private stage school. He said, 'If you're upstaged, allow it that once. If you're upstaged again at the next house, be wary. If it happens a third time – move down.'

Even the nicest people can be a bit naughty sometimes. Once I had a funny scene with a very famous comedian, where I was telling him about my son scoring the goal for some crummy football team. I had a veil on my hat, with felt rings as big as shillings all over it. As I was talking I would get this veil caught in my mouth, and have to blow it out before I could go on. As long as you don't overdo it, that sort of thing always gets a good laugh. Some nights you could have done two rows of knitting while the laugh went on. One night this famous comic moved up a yard during my speech. It means the audience only sees one side of your face, which is not as funny. I did nothing. The next night he moved two yards upstage. I still did nothing, but I wasn't getting anything like the laugh I'd had before.

On the second house, I moved down as he moved up. I was nearly in the footlights, but everyone in the audience could see my face. As I came off he was waiting for me. He said, 'There's not much anyone can teach you about comedy, is there?'

I said, 'Not about the dirty work, there isn't. I know all the tricks that go on. I haven't used any on you, so you can stop it!'

It kills your laugh, when somebody is doing something to distract the audience during your line. Even an actor clearing his throat, 'Ahem!' will kill a laugh if they do it on the word in the line that's funny. I couldn't be bothered with it, but a lot of comics I've known would stop at nothing to prevent another comic from getting a laugh. It's nearly amusing, when you're an artist, watching them trying to kill a laugh, especially when it doesn't come off.

Often it is the rhythm of the speech that gets the laughs, not just the words. My father taught me that. He used to say, 'It's music, is comedy.' It's the timing of the gesture, or the rhythm of the language. Sometimes you don't even need words. If somebody's saying something, and you're listening, you can say anything you like with your face. You can say, 'Hey, wait a minute!' Without saying a word, just with your face. Everyone can see you are asking yourself, 'Whatever is she saying?'

The plays of Eden Phillpotts were very popular in the days I was starting out in rep. I don't know if you are familiar with them. We used to do about seven or eight of his plays a year in Morecambe. I had nothing to do in one, no words to learn, only to be a kid of about ten – I was only seven stone, so that was easy. I had long hair in those days, and whenever I had to play a schoolgirl, Jimmy would cut about two inches off the bottom and stick it together with Sellotape and make it into a fringe. I put a beret on top of that. So in my twenties I was playing maids, schoolgirls and grand-mothers. But I don't like to be on stage and not get a laugh when it's a comedy. Bert Oakes was the director and I said to him, 'Have I to do anything, Mr Oakes?' Because it's sometimes a bit difficult to know what to do with yourself when you've to be on stage with nothing to say.

And he said, 'No, no . . . Well, all right – have an apple. Eat an apple.'

I always ate an apple like a chipmunk, nibbling round and round the core with tiny little bites. I still do. So I set off, sitting on a stool, eating this apple – nothing to say or anything, just going round and round the core. And you could hear people beginning to murmur in the audience, 'Oh, look – ha-ha!' 'Ho! Ho!' And that starts an audience off, one or two people getting the giggles.

The rest of the cast didn't like it – and they were right not to. I was guilty of what I've just said some other comics did. I was distracting the audience. (But I got my laugh!)

In another Eden Phillpotts play I wore a bunch of cherries hanging off the brim of my hat, playing someone sitting on one of those benches that go round a tree. It was a non-speaking part. An actor called Mr Roberts had to sit behind me on this circular seat. Well, I have to admit that my cherries did hide him a bit from the audience, considering he had some lines and I hadn't. He would hunch down to be seen under these cherries, or he would stretch up to look over the top, or he would try to knock them out of the way. On the Saturday night, the last night, he came on stage with a pair of scissors in his pocket, which he took out, cut my cherries off and chucked them away. That got a laugh all right.

Not in the Diary

You did a lot of daft things in rep.

My mother was once singing a love duet with Carey Cowell, and she said to him, 'I do wish you'd clean your teeth or something before you come on. The beer smell is terrible – it's putting me off.'

But he wouldn't, so the next time my mother bit the top off a bunch of spring onions and chewed them before she went on. There she was, singing 'I love you,' gazing up into his face and Carey Cowell was nearly fainting with the pong.

Gladys Cooper was another one. I never worked with her but, oh, she was clever. My understudy, Connie Merrigold, was with me for fourteen years. Then she got her first proper part in the West End – I mean, not as an understudy. In the play Connie's got a plate of sandwiches and she has to eat one just after she says her funny line. Gladys Cooper would 'accidentally on purpose' knock the sandwich off the plate and then pick it up again. She used to time it exactly so that she was picking it up just as Connie was saying her funny line. So she got the laugh instead of Connie. This had been going on for about four nights when she told me about it. I wasn't in the play, but I had called backstage to see her and ask how she was getting on with Miss Cooper. She said, 'I don't think she's noticed I'm in it. Oh yes, she has. Because she kills my one funny line by doing some business with the sandwich.' And she told me what happened.

'Oh, that old trick,' I said. 'I'll tell you what you do. Wait until she's just making her exit, and then pick the sandwich up again from the plate, give it a look and instead of eating it, throw it down yourself. That'll get you a laugh.' It did. A big one.

Fay Compton was a lovely actress, a really wonderful actress. But I've always thought it was such a pity that both Fay Compton and Gladys Cooper, who were known by all England as great ladies of the theatre, could be so jealous and petty. Please believe me – I'm not saying they weren't great actresses. They were. But they did have this jealousy thing.

Fay Compton was jealous of me, even when she was the leading lady and I was only playing her char. I rarely came off without getting a note from her, because I was getting laughs she didn't think I should get. Fay didn't give you many notes herself, but she gave them to you through the stage director. I used to scratch my back, just as I went off, and it used to get a laugh and a round of applause for my exit. George Brody, the stage director, came up to me one day. 'Miss Compton says you are to cut that scratch. She doesn't like it.'

I said, 'But it always gets a big laugh.'

'It wasn't in the play. Cut it. And don't put anything else in.'

During the run, Fay's new husband ran off with a Canadian actress, Patricia Roc – a name that will probably mean nothing to you now, unless you watch the old movies on afternoon television. At one time

Rank had about twenty young starlets under contract – we called them 'Mr Rank's pound-a-weekers' – and they included Jean Kent and Pat Roc.

Fay had come back from her honeymoon to start work on *No Medals*, which was a big West End hit and we ran for three years during the war. My Jimmy was in the RAF, and he had said to me, 'If we're going abroad, I'll leave you a message, "The brown boots fit" if I can get to a telephone.' And one day George, the doorkeeper, rang my dressing-room to say I was wanted on the telephone – quick. So I ran down the hall and Jimmy said, 'Darling, the brown boots fit. God bless you and Jan.'

Boom. Phone down. That was it. I'd no time to say, 'I love you', or 'Come home safely', or anything.

I went to the side of the stage ready to go on, feeling a bit sad. George the doorkeeper must have told Miss Compton about my telephone conversation, and just as I was about to go on, she said to me, quite kindly, 'I believe your husband has gone abroad and left you on your own.'

Unfortunately I said, 'Oh yes. But I'm not the only one am I, Miss Compton?' Because I didn't know that the *Evening News* had just come out with a big picture of Fay's husband, with the headline that he had run off with Pat Roc. I was meaning, of course, that many women's husbands were being sent overseas. But what a thing to say to her!

She said, 'No – you're not the only one. And he hasn't left you for a chorus girl, has he?'

I had no idea what she was talking about. And then it was my entrance so I had to go on. I was sharing a dressing-room with Robin Cole. One of the best things I've ever done in my life. A beautiful woman. More men than I've had cups of tea! Room full of flowers. And she'd say, 'I wonder which one those are from!'

As soon as I came off-stage I went and told her about the telephone call. I said, 'Oh, Robin, it was Jimmy. He said the brown boots fitted.' She knew what that meant. She hugged me up. She was a darling.

Then I told her about the funny conversation with Miss Compton just before I went on. She said, 'Well, you're *not* the only one. He's left her.'

I said, 'Who has left who?'

She said, 'Michael' – or whatever his name was – 'has gone off with Pat Roc.'

I'm afraid that was the only time I felt sorry for Fay Compton.

So many things come back to me as though they happened yesterday. I don't as a rule suffer too much from 'corpsing' – the desire to laugh at an inappropriate moment. But it did happen to me once.

I was in a beautiful play called *Mrs Moonlight*. I played Sarah – the maid, of course – and in the first act there was a firescreen, with a padded seat on the top. I was sitting knitting with six fine knitting needles because – as any woman will know, or perhaps not nowadays – you used to knit socks that way. And you can hear her going click, click, click, click, click, click. In Act 2 it's a rather smaller firescreen and the needles are a little bit bigger. In Act 3 they were those great big wooden needles. Sarah the maid opens every act sitting there, with her knitting.

Norman Hammond, who was the leading man, had a big soliloquy at the beginning of the last act. He always used to walk rather grandly to centre stage to start it, and it began with something like, 'In days of old when knights were bold . . .'

One night, just as he started his soliloquy, a dog someone had smuggled into the audience woke up and began to yap. It was in the stalls somewhere. Norman carried on, but every time he tried to speak this dog started up yapping and growling, and the owner was saying, 'Shhhh. Sit. Come here.'

About halfway through his speech Norman stopped, I can see him now, in his white-hosed outfit, putting his hands behind his back as he glared down into the audience and said, 'Take that dog out!'

Nothing to do with the play, but he said it. Now, I was there with those big wooden knitting needles, my hands shaking, trying not to laugh. We heard the noise of a theatre seat going up – you can always recognise that thump - and the woman had put the dog in her coat, and it was going 'Grrrr, grrrrh!' and they were leaving.

Norman was standing there, shouting, 'That's right! Take it out. Take it right out.'

He was furious. She walked up the side, and as she

Dinnerladies: Thora Hird with Victoria Wood and
David Roper, November 1994

Dame Thora talks to Paul Daniels at the Royal Marsden
Cancer Appeal, January 1997

Dame Thora celebrates after being hailed 'Oldie of
the Year' at the Oldie of the Year Awards, February 1999

The *Parkinson Show*: Dame Thora takes centre-stage
with Michael Parkinson and Jim Davidson, February 1999

Dame Thora celebrates her 88th birthday with Help the Aged, May 1999

Dame Thora with the Emmy Award presented to *Lost for Words* for
Best International Drama, New York, November 1999

The *Lost for Words* team celebrate their triumph on Emmy night:
Thora Hird with Alan Bell and Keith Richardson, November 1999

Dame Thora arriving at the Royal Albert Hall with Des Lynam
for the Comedy of the Year Awards where *Last of the Summer Wine*
was presented with the Royal Television Society Best
Comedy Series Award, November 1999

was going out of the double swing-doors at the back the dog got caught in one, and let out such a yowl.

Norman said, 'Thank you', and then he strode to centre stage and started his soliloquy all over again, right from the beginning. That's what finished me. I had to drop my ball of wool to get myself behind the settee, because I was quaking with laughing. I lay behind this settee clutching my sides, and I couldn't come back out until the end of the soliloquy, because every time I thought about it I started to laugh again.

'I can't blame you,' he said to me afterwards. 'Dogs in the theatre – they'll bring their giraffes in next.'

Then there was the great Arthur Askey. I was with Arthur in *The Love Match*, at Victoria Palace. Suddenly there was this loud noise – *crick, crack* – coming from some people in the front of the stalls who were shelling nuts. Crick, crack, crick, crack. Arthur stopped in the middle of a speech, leaned over and said, 'Have you nearly finished with those? Pass us up a couple, will you, while we're waiting? Because you're louder than we are!'

A lot of what I do, I've seen for nothing. I've always watched people. I watched people so much and for so long when I was working in the Co-op that I'm still using things I noticed then in the parts I play now. I always watch people in the street, I watch them in the shops, I watch someone doing something funny and I think, 'I'll library that for it coming up some day.' At the top of the mews where I live there's a pub on the corner. You could sit at one of the tables outside and watch the street and see enough in an hour to be able to keep acting character parts for a lifetime.

One day I was invited to a service at St Martin in the Fields, in Trafalgar Square. I'd arrived a bit early, so I sat at the back. The organist was practising, and the church was quite full of people – all tramps. Some of them were taking a nap. You could hear the snores. A few pews in front of me sat an old woman with two big plastic bags beside her – all she owned in her life. As it got near to the time for people to arrive for the next service the sidesmen walked down the aisles quietly asking all the tramps to leave, so they could get the church ready. I watched the old lady gather up her bags and shuffle off down the aisle to the front of the church. Then she shuffled all the way round to the back of the church down the far aisle, and went out of one of the doors at the back . . . and then came back in again through the other door behind me and sat back down again. By this time all the sidesmen were busy doing something else and nobody saw all this but me. I thought to myself, 'I'll play you one day.' I will too.

In my own way I think I work the same way that Alan Bennett does. I observe people and I remember the small details of the things they do – a movement of the hand or a way of sitting down can tell you so much about a person. Whether they are confident or nervous, aggressive or gentle. He writes it down in his brilliant plays, but one of the reasons that his plays are so good is because they are so well observed about ordinary people.

A woman walking along stopping to scratch herself. You might think, 'Nobody would do that.' But yes they do. I've seen it. And I've copied it – and it gets a laugh because the audience recognises it.

It's interesting playing the part of a person who is very pleased to see you and then has a drink, and you see a different woman at the end of it. 'No, well, just a drop. I don't take it often. Thank you very much.'

Friendly and pleasant as anything when they arrive. Quarrelsome bloody know-all after one sherry! A lot of people write a play in five minutes. It's a fact.

'No, it isn't!'

I was doing *Saturday Night at the Crown* at Blackpool, a play the great Walter Greenwood wrote for me, and it was full of laughs that show, all the way through. In it I am sitting at a small table with my husband, Herbert. My character says in her drunk scene, 'That Mr Khrushchev. He come over. Come to the mill – I got you them socks for then, do you remember, Herbert?'

That line was one laugh. Then he uncrosses his legs, with his boots on, and a pair of dreadful, bright, luminous pink socks shows over the top.

In another scene I had to eat a pork pie. The barmaid

says, 'Same as usual, 'Erbert?' and I call over, 'And a pie, while you're at it.'

So Herbert brings me the pie. On the Tuesday in Bradford, I put this next bit in at rehearsal. I said to Walter Greenwood, 'Go in front and watch this, and if you don't want it, we'll leave it out. But I've thought of something.'

I carefully broke the pie in half. Now if you divide a bought pork pie, you can break the crust exactly in half. But the meat stays oval, all in one piece. Just the crust breaks. So I divided it exactly – and then gave Herbert half the crust bit, and kept all the meat for myself. That was one big laugh. But then a tiny bit of meat fell out on the floor. I picked it up and wiped it on my coat, got his crust back, put the meat in and gave it back to him. (Perhaps you need to have lived through rationing to appreciate how funny it was.)

One night there was the usual laughter, and then I heard a sort of 'Ooh, ooh!' sound coming from the stalls. It came very near the interval and during the interval one of the checkers, the girls who take you to your seats, came round to my dressing-room and said, 'Miss Hird, I'm sorry about the disturbance.'

I said, 'What was it? Was somebody taken ill?'

She said, 'No. But a lady in the upper circle laughed so much that her teeth fell out. And they landed on the head of the only bald-headed man in the pit. And he cried out. So I'm afraid there's a little bit of disturbance at the moment, while my girls look for the teeth.'

Two laughs for one

So that's how funny you can be – so funny people's teeth fall out.

Number Ten

September 1999

14 September 10 Downing Street Reception for Stroke Association

Tony Blair is the third Prime Minister I've met at receptions held at Number Ten. The first time I was invited there, it must be ten years ago now, was when Mrs Thatcher was Prime Minister. It was in April.

At the Methodist Central Hall, Westminster, they have a Daffodil Day every year usually either in March or April, to celebrate new life, when the whole place is decorated with a great mass of daffodils – all the balconies and everything. The flowers get taken round to hospitals and old people's homes afterwards. I often went there to speak on Daffodil Day, especially when our very dear friend, Rev. John Tudor, who has recently retired, was the minister. Two thousand women come, from Women's Institutes all over the country. It's lovely to meet them, and it's silly to say that you know two thousand people, but I *feel* I know them.

On this particular occasion, ten years ago, John Tudor knew that I was going on to see Mrs Thatcher later that day. I think the Prime Minister usually gave about four of these special receptions a year. John Tudor knows Mrs Thatcher, a fellow Methodist, so he said to me, 'Will you take her these daffodils for her? And give her a message from me?'

I said, 'With pleasure.'

Scottie and I walked over to Number Ten, and one of the secretaries at the entrance saw us come in with an armful of flowers so I told her that they were for Mrs Thatcher. She said, 'Well, give them to me, and I'll put them in a bucket of water for now, and arrange them later.'

When I was introduced to Mrs Thatcher, I told her that John Tudor and all the Methodists from the Central Hall had sent her daffodils for Daffodil Day, that were downstairs. She said to me, 'They are such good people.'

I also passed on the message from John Tudor. He had told me to tell her to 'not work too hard, because we all love her!' She laughed when I told her, but you could tell there were tears there, too.

We were talking about our busy lives, and she told me that she never failed to write her 'thank you' notes on the same day – even after a late evening – before she went to bed. What a great idea – the events of the evening are still fresh in your mind, and your letter ready for the post when you get up in the morning, so it doesn't get forgotten or postponed by the events of a busy day. Not to mention the fact that the sooner it arrives, the more it will mean to its recipient.

Some people thought of Maggie Thatcher as an 'Iron

Lady', and in some ways that may even have helped her in her difficult role as Prime Minister in our funny old world. But there was another side to her, as anyone who met her could tell you, or anyone who saw her in one particular television interview when I saw there were tears in her eyes as she talked about her much-loved father.

I've always known that under that efficient, business-like exterior there beat the heart of a real woman. Scottie and I remarked to one another at the time how strange, but nice, it was to see her taking such a pride and joy in showing us round Number Ten, which had all been newly redecorated. She was as proud as any woman would be showing off her home to guests.

When it was time to leave it was pouring with rain outside, like it so often does in April. We'd walked there in the sunshine, and I'd no coat and, of course, for security reasons, taxis and cars aren't allowed to drive down Downing Street for ordinary members of the public. There were about three security officers just inside the front door. I said, 'Oh, good gracious, look at it.'

One of these policemen said, 'Well, I think we can send for a taxi to come to the door, as it's you.'

So Scottie and I were driven away down Downing Street in style, and straight home to write our letter of thanks to a gracious hostess for a lovely evening.

The second time I went to Number Ten was equally

enjoyable. Jan and I were invited to a reception a few years later, by John and Norma Major. This time it was a lovely summer evening and the reception was held in the garden. If you want my honest opinion, the garden was a bit disappointing as gardens go. Perhaps all the 'instant' gardening programmes we see on television nowadays have spoiled us all? The garden at Number Ten was rather bare, with very little planted, and not much imagination about what there was. Jan and I put it down to 'security'. You can't have intruders hiding behind a big bush, can you?

Norma Major was smiling sweetly in the receiving line to welcome everybody as we all entered through the rose garden, but I think she must have nipped off home to put John's dinner on straight after, because when I was looking for her later, she'd already left. I was rather sorry, because I wanted to congratulate her on the excellent reviews I had read of her book about Chequers. I love any book that's about real-life history.

Instead I found myself chatting to someone I'd always wanted to meet and never had until then, the brilliant choreographer of ballet, Anthony Dowell. I'm lost in admiration for people who can do what he does – and he seemed thrilled to meet me too! I often think how lucky I am to meet people from so many different walks of life. And I met Matthew Parris, the journalist from *The Times*, who had once been an MP and one of Mrs Thatcher's personal assistants. He told me he had just been talking to someone else for half an hour who he had been convinced was me, so he'd been telling them what a fan he was, and about all the things he'd seen me in. He was now wondering whoever it could have been, and whatever they thought he was talking about!

Next I found an old friend, Ken Dodd. He takes his politics very seriously, does Ken, but I got him off his soapbox and round to talking about the good old times we had shared in Blackpool doing the summer seasons. He began his professional life under the stage name of Professor Yaffle Chuckabutty – Operatic Tenor and Sausage Knotter. They were great days for us, the fifties and sixties, with marvellous comics, the Crazy Gang, Monsewer Eddie Gray, Jimmy James and Arthur Askey, as well as the new boys on the block . . . Tommy Cooper, Des O'Connor and Morecambe and Wise.

Ten live shows there used to be in Blackpool, in the summer, with 1,400 artists, including the lines of dancing girls. Everyone used to come to Blackpool for their holidays. Straight from the station and into Yates's Wine Lodge. You'd see lines of luggage outside Yates's, because they didn't get as far as their digs. Sherry – sixpence. Champagne – elevenpence. There were many gags about Yates's Wine Lodge: They always put the cab fare to go home behind the clock in their digs. There weren't as many hotels then. Most people stayed in lodgings. Behind the clock went the cab fare, as soon as they arrived, so they could spend everything else and still have enough to get home.

In Church Street, where I was at the Grand – it doesn't

mean the grandest theatre – there was the Grand, the Winter Gardens, the Opera House, and the Hippodrome. They all came out after first house at the same time. Church Street couldn't hold all the people. So the Blackpool Watch Committee used to come round and say, 'Could you cut four minutes out this week?'

Ken Dodd never would cut anything out – I don't think he'd have known how. So when he was there, I'd have to, or one of the others. The next week Morecambe and Wise at the Hippodrome would cut out a bit, so we'd all finish at different times. The crowds were like Piccadilly Circus in the rush hour, half trying to get out of the theatres, and half queuing to come in for the second house.

Ken is in the *Guinness Book of Records* for telling 1,500 jokes non-stop in three and a half hours. It doesn't surprise me. Once, at the Opera House in Blackpool, when Ken was top of the bill, the entire orchestra packed up and left before he came on as the final act. The management had told them they were not going to be paid overtime if Ken got carried away and stayed on stage too long – which to the delight of the audiences, he always did!

But I digress. We are still in Downing Street. Later John Major himself came up to say hello to Jan and me, and was delightful and we found that everything we'd heard about him was true – his real personality never comes across on TV. 'In the flesh' he is a charmer. He admired my tiny Union Jack brooch with 'Great Britain' written on it, which I was wearing as I very often do. He wanted to know where he could get one and laughed when I suddenly remembered where I had bought it – Hong Kong!

Ten years after my first visit to Number Ten, I was there again last September. Number Ten has wheelchair access – a ramp was put down for me in ten seconds flat, and inside there is a stairlift – known in some circles as a 'Thora Hird' these days – as well as an ordinary lift. Unfortunately, that day I needed it.

Cherie was there to welcome us and told us that the Government redecorates Number Ten every ten years, so it had just been done again. She seemed very happy and genuinely pleased to see us. It was rather a pleasure to see her take the same pride in the redecoration that Maggie had done ten years before. (Ten years ago – I can't believe it.) Now the main reception room had been painted a light colour and the columns had been drag-painted to look like marble. She showed us how the pictures of generals and battles and 'other dull things' have all gone and been replaced by a huge painting of the ballerina Darcey Bussell, in pink and yellow. There's a rather hard-faced portrait of P.D. James, whose detective stories Jan and I both enjoy. Over the fireplace I noticed with great pleasure a small portrait of Sir Dirk Bogarde, God rest him. The pleasure his books have brought to Jan and me. *Once a Jolly Swagman* was his very first film and I played his mother in it. I think I might *just* have been ten years older than him! They quite often show it on television. There is also a portrait of Kazuo Ishiguro, the author of *Remains of the Day*. I haven't read the book, but the film needs at least one box of Kleenex.

Tony Blair arrived very late. He had come straight from giving his long speech at the TUC Conference at Brighton. He said to me, 'Hallo! What are you doing here?'

I said, 'It's private. I'm not supposed to tell you.'

Tony's father, Leo, had a stroke when he was only young. Tony himself had been nine at the time. It took his father three years to learn to speak again. Tony said it changes not only your own life, but everyone in your family's life, forever. So he had had no hesitation when asked by the Stroke Association if they could hold this reception at Number Ten. Cherie said, 'We don't want to think of it as "our" house – it is everybody's house.'

As we were leaving I said to Tony, because he had arrived so late after making his long speech, 'Too long for twice nightly in Blackpool, that speech of yours. You'll have to cut it.'

He didn't see the joke, so I just said, 'Well, I hope Cherie has put your dinner in the oven to keep warm.'

I see from my diary that the next time I saw them both was at the Speaker's reception for the Queen's opening of Parliament in November 1999. What isn't in the diary is that Jan and I both remarked on how beautiful Cherie was looking. She had a lovely glow about her. And now, of course, we all know the reason why . . .

.

Among the donkeys

September 1999

28 September Open Elisabeth Svendsen's donkey sanctuary, Leeds 11.00 a.m.

In September last year I did something that I really love doing, and that is opening a donkey sanctuary in Leeds. I've always had a soft spot for these gentle creatures.

The last time I was at a donkey sanctuary must have been more than ten years ago, when I was doing *Praise Be!* I visited the one at Sidmouth, where they have over five thousand donkeys. Can you believe it? Many of them have been rescued from being cruelly treated or neglected. And it's not just for the donkeys. The point is that little disabled children can learn to ride on them. You see, it's a gentle little thing is a donkey. It doesn't race about. Where a pony or a horse might be too big and frightening for a small child, a little donkey is just right.

When I went to Sidmouth I did something that I have wanted to do all my life – I drove a donkey cart. I was with a film crew, of course, and they used the film of it every Sunday on *Praise Be!* in the opening titles. Elisabeth Svendsen, who runs the sanctuary, told me that one donkey was having a baby that night, and if it was a girl she wanted to call it Thora, would I mind? But it was a boy, dark grey, like a storm cloud, so she called it Thor instead. He'll be a big boy now.

When I was a child, we used to be playing round the clock on the promenade at Morecambe after school, and in the summer the sands were full of visitors having donkey rides. There was a stone ramp – we called it the 'ramper' – built of stones, making a path up from the sands to the promenade. Every evening the donkey men used to bring the donkeys up it, their little feet tapping on the stone ramper, after their hard day's work on the sands. The donkeys all had their names written on their bridles, Silver and Neddy and Jacko. We used to run along beside them along the road as they trotted home, after giving pleasure all day. You don't wonder Jesus chose to ride one, do you?

When I got to Leeds last September to open the new sanctuary, I was delighted to find that they were going to put on a production of *Cinderella* for us, with handicapped children acting the story, all riding on the donkeys. There was a paddock in the middle, with seats all round for us to watch. First lots of little donkeys came tripping on. A beautiful sight. Some were cream, and some were fawn, some were chocolate brown. There was someone at either side of each donkey – in other words, on either side of each child – and someone else leading it. The children riding them were all in different-coloured jodhpurs and each had an envelope the same

colour as their riding clothes. At the far end was a row
of letterboxes to match the colour of the envelopes and
their jodhpurs, and if a child managed to post a red
envelope, say, in the red letterbox, they got a round of
applause.

Then they went off and another little child toddled
on wearing a shawl, and sat down in the middle. She
might have been three. Not more than five, anyway. She
was Cinderella. There was no talking or commentary,
but there was music, and you could tell what was
happening. It was a real pantomime. First there was a
procession of beautiful donkeys, with the prince in front,
a little boy, beautifully dressed, silver paper across his
riding hat and his donkey had silver all round his
headband, like a little crown. Then he and the others in
the procession all go by, ignoring the little girl. She
looks at him, the prince, but he just rides away, so she is
shunned. She looked so upset.

Then the little girl went off, and came back on again
with one of the attendants dressed up as the dame, and
two others as ugly sisters, and there was a bit of funny
pantomime with them.

Then it was the ball scene. Eventually Cinders comes
on in a little pink net dress to the ball. The prince comes
up to her on his donkey. By now people were nearly
weeping. Well, I *was* weeping, never mind nearly. We
hadn't been able to take our eyes off this little girl. Then
she ran out and I was wondering, 'Where did the slipper
go?'

The next scene was the prince going round trying to find his Cinderella, and they had the best idea that I've ever seen in my life, I think. Instead of a glass slipper the prince and his followers have got a little silver horseshoe – or donkey shoe. They go round to all the donkeys and put it against their feet, but it doesn't fit any of them. And then the prince comes to the little donkey belonging to Cinders and lifts up its leg to try it on, and of course that's where you get 'It fits! It fits!' And this little child is laughing round at everyone, as if to say, 'Have you seen the joke?'

Then they put her on the donkey and off she goes.

The last scene was the walk-down, with the two children on their donkeys leading. There was not a dry eye in the house. We were all sniffling. And they rode off to an ovation, she with a riding hat on with a bit of silver-and-pink tassel tied round to show she was a princess. It was the most magic thing. It did me good. I said afterwards to Elisabeth Svendsen, 'When will you ever think of anything better than that?'

She said, 'When we've got another £440,000 we're opening another one in Manchester. Will you come and open it?'

I said, 'May God let me live that long.'

Oldies

February 1999

I never feel old. Like most old people, I feel just the same as I have always done. But I have to admit that recently one of the few places I've been to where I was probably not the oldest person present was when I was invited by the editor of the *Oldie* magazine to Simpson's in the Strand for their annual 'Oldie of the Year' lunch. I was their 'Oldie of the Year' for 1998 – well, nobody envies you that, because nobody will admit they're old enough. It's not something most people would want to boast about.

In 1998 Jan came with me, and there must have been two or three hundred guests – politicians, writers, actors and people from all walks of life – of which I would think about a third were genuine 'oldies'. And that was a bit daft because after we had all had drinks in the bar downstairs, when it was time to go in to lunch it was three floors up – and no lift. Simpson's is so old that Charles Dickens used to eat there – so no lift. Larry Adler was telling me that he had been at this same luncheon the previous year and when he got to the top of the stairs, 'I fainted dead away, dear!'

As soon as he told me this, we looked at one another, and two minds with but a single thought, we started up the stairs together, well ahead of the others. We heaved our way slowly to the top, without either of us fainting I'm glad to say, and we were sitting in our places looking dignified and calm by the time the others appeared, huffing and puffing and all red in the face.

At the top table I sat with Spike Milligan and Ludovic Kennedy who had both won awards and made very funny speeches. I was presented with my 'Oldie of the Year' award by Mr Roy Hattersley, who was standing in at the last minute for Betty Boothroyd, who had been called away to the House of Commons. She had won the Disciplinarian of the Year prize. Ludovic Kennedy had won the Old Campaigner of the Year award, and in his speech he asked us all to commit euthanasia, which he does at the drop of a hat. (I don't mean he commits euthanasia at the drop of the hat – I mean he makes speeches suggesting that we *all* should at the drop of a hat.) Humphrey Lyttelton and Jimmy Young were both Survivors of the Year. Richard Whiteley, from *Countdown* – which I love – was sitting next to Jan. He won the 'Most Inexplicable Survivor of the Year' award. And Mavis Nicholson had won something else. So it was a very splendid occasion. There was plenty of wine and good conversation, and a good time was had by all.

I saw another old friend further down the table, Barry Cryer, one of our best and funniest actors, and one the nicest people in the world you could know. Now here's a little story that shows the older you get, the dafter you get. It must be ten years ago, easily, that we met when we worked together for some charity thing, and afterwards he'd written me a letter and it was Christmas-time, so he'd put a Christmas card in with it. After I'd read the letter I'd torn it up, like I do when I've read the mail, and put it in the wastepaper bucket. Not because I hated him. My desk is like a car boot sale as it is, I get so many letters, so after I've read them I always chuck them away. But then I wanted to send him a Christmas card, and I thought, 'But what's his address?' Then I remembered I'd torn it up. So I went through the bucket and found the ten pieces. It took me about quarter of an hour to stick them all together again, to get the address.

So I wrote to him and told him what I'd done. But knowing what a funny man he is, I thought I'd tear my own reply up and mend it again with Sellotape before sending it to him. And that's gone on for ten or twelve years – if he writes to me about anything, the letter has always been torn up and stuck together again. I mean, the time it takes us to do this!

So at the 1999 lunch I could see Barry Cryer at one of the tables, sitting next to Barry Took. The last course of this meal was roly-poly pudding, and I must admit it was nearly as good as my mother's. So I got the little place card, with my name on it, and I wrote, 'What do you think of the pud? Will recommend?' (Old theatrical pros always used to put this, if they had a landlady at their digs who was a good cook: 'Good pud. Will recommend.')

Then I tore the card up into little bits like you've never seen, called the waiter over and said, 'Would you give this to Mr Cryer down there, please.'

The waiter looked at it and said, 'It's all torn up.'

I said, 'Yes. I know. It's difficult to explain it to you. Just take it to him, will you?'

I watched him go down, but pretended not to be watching, while the waiter handed Barry all these bits of card. In a bit the waiter was back with another plate full of little bits. When I got them together I saw Barry had written, 'What's it got to do with you?'

And there we were, grown-ups – *oldies* – doing all this. Good gracious, I'm a grandmother. But it's very nice to be silly sometimes. It does you good.

Towards the end of this very traditional English meal, a schoolboy feast with heavy puddings, Lord Longford, who was sitting across from Jan at the top table, leaned across and said to her, 'I don't believe we have been introduced?'

She said, 'No, indeed, but of course I know who *you* are, Lord Longford.'

She told him who she was, and that she was my daughter. He said something very nice and took her hand to kiss it, then he slowly bowed his head down over her hand, laid it on the table, using it as a little pillow and fell fast asleep. It was that sort of a lunch. Richard Whiteley, who was sitting next to Jan, tittered, but Jan says she is sure that nobody else even noticed. She didn't know what to do. His head was quite heavy, and she didn't want to pull her hand away suddenly to wake him up and embarrass him. But after a few minutes he woke up again by himself. He was quite refreshed and not at all aware that time had stood still for a few moments. Who could blame him? The room was full of smoke by then, and we'd all enjoyed a very big lunch.

There is a real problem for people like myself, going to these lunches, especially if they want you to speak at the end. They will come up behind you and 'top up' your wine glass. It's quite wrong, and very unfair. I only ever want one glass of wine. The trouble is, if you are in full flight, talking and enjoying yourself, and the meal takes a long time, you don't notice that you have had the equivalent of nearly three glasses by the time coffee arrives. I must confess that I was feeling more than ready to join Lord Longford in a little nap rather than make a witty speech at the end of that particular meal.

But then Larry Adler took out his harmonica and was joined by Humphrey Lyttelton on the trumpet for a small traditional jazz jam session. Soon all our toes were tapping and nobody felt a bit old.

'Onward Christian soldiers'

December 1997

Lunch on the Orient Express

If you know me, you might know that 'Onward
Christian soldiers' has always been my favourite hymn,
ever since I was a little girl collecting the tea cakes for
my mother on a Saturday night, when the local Salvation Army band would be playing outside Dora's
confectionery shop. Dora did her second baking at six,
so you could have your tea cakes still fresh for Sunday.
Happy Jack, one of the Morecambe fishermen, would
always be there in his little hat and blue *ganzie* – our
Morecambe word for a Guernsey sweater. His voice
was so loud they could have heard him across the bay
at Grange when he sang 'Onward Christian soldiers'. I
always waited for that before running home. My mother
used to say, 'Get us the tea cakes for tomorrow,
Thora . . . and don't stay too long singing with the
Sally Army.' But I never left until Happy Jack had sung
'Onward Christian soldiers'.

When I was doing *Praise Be!* I visited Horbury Bridge
in Yorkshire, where Sabine Baring-Gould first composed 'Onward Christian soldiers' in 1864, when he

was curate-in-charge. He wrote it for the children to sing on their Sunday school's annual Whit Sunday procession when they had to march to the next village for a united service. He couldn't find anything suitable for them to march to, so he wrote something himself. The tune and the words are both very good for marching, and I taught it to my grandchildren, Daisy and James, when they were small children growing up in America, to introduce them to the very English delights of long country walks. As long as we were all singing 'Onward Christian soldiers' I could keep them marching along.

I don't do much marching as to war myself these days. I can't get out of my chair without help. But it's only a couple of years since Rev. Rob Marshall organised several pilgrimages for Scottie, Jan and me to go on, to walk in our sandals to all the places where Jesus and his disciples had walked. It's the most wonderful experience for a Christian. I still hope I might go on one more, if God is willing.

Rob Marshall is a dear friend who often drops in to see me for a coffee at the mews. We first met when I interviewed his boss, Rt. Rev. David Hope for *Praise Be!* when he was Bishop of London. Of course, now David Hope is even more important – Archbishop of York. What a leading man! He could have made his fortune as a film star. Rob was his chaplain and public relations adviser, and they are still great friends – with each other and with me.

As I've said, these days Rob is the Vicar of St Augustine's, South Kensington. I go to a lot of their dos, and I've been on a few church outings with the parish. It's not quite the same as going on pilgrimage, but we are all 'onward Christians', and always have a most interesting time. They have made me so welcome there, and it's like being part of a big church family. They have a turkey dinner at Christmas, and I've been to that.

Two Christmases ago Rob and his churchwarden, Sue MacDonald, who organises all the church outings and things, arranged the most wonderful treat for me. Rob telephoned me one day in early December and said, 'How would you like to have a Christmas lunch on the *Orient Express*? Have you ever been on it?'

I said, 'Yes. No.'

I met Rob and Sue and her husband at St Augustine's – there were just the four of us going. We boarded the *Orient Express* in the morning, which took us to Ramsgate and then – I don't mean it literally did this – it turned round and came back to Victoria at about four in the afternoon.

There were lots of people on the train, but we had our own private carriage, for the four of us, which was so beautiful it was as good as the Queen's carriage. I've never seen anything like it. The waiters were all in white livery with gilt braid, and the food – ooh! Marvellous. They had three musicians going up and down the train, all seventy if they were a minute, playing a baby banjo, saxophone and clarinet, so there was music all the way. We had tremendous Christmas crackers with gifts and exotic paper hats in them. And the drink! Champagne. Whatever you wanted. A huge tray of brandies and liqueurs with the coffee. We could all have been drunk before we even left Victoria – but of course we weren't.

The band kept coming to the door of our carriage and asking, 'What shall we play now, Thora? "Ain't She Sweet"?' And off they'd go. We had music all the way and all the way back. So that was my Christmas treat that year – to go puff-puffing.

April 1998

Marching as to Wales

The following spring the whole parish of St Augustine's went on a coach outing to Wales for the day, and invited me along. A member of the congregation is Pamela Thomas OBE, who is a barrister, but I always call her the Baroness, because she's very grand, rather bossy and much larger than life so she really ought to be at least a baroness. I just love her. So now we're 'the Baroness and the Dame'. She has a beautiful Queen Anne house in Wales and invited the church to have a parish outing to come and have lunch with her there.

I thought we were never going to arrive. I kept saying, 'When are we going to get there?'

And Sue MacDonald, who had made all the arrangements, would say, 'Just a minute' as she peered through the pages of her itinerary, and then she'd say, 'I should think in about a quarter of an hour.'

An hour after that she was saying to the driver, 'Where are we now?'

In the end it was five hours on the coach and I must admit it was partly because of me that it took so long. We would call at a motorway pull-in, where everybody stops for coffee and toffees and things, to get petrol. The Ladies was full of ladies and I was *surrounded* for autographs. Afterwards I was making for the coach, and as soon as one person stopped me, I was quickly surrounded again. It kept everybody waiting while I signed road-maps and envelopes and all sorts of scraps of paper thrust at me, but what can you do?

We arrived eventually. And it was quite a comedy, when we did get there, to find this elegant Queen Anne house, and the Baroness standing at the gate, with an apron on, 'You're an hour late, I suppose you know this?'

Poor Sue was in disgrace all day long, because of our arriving so late. Then it was, 'Have you brought the Dame? Where's Thora?'

Her footmen were wearing jeans and sweaters. Lunch was served in the kitchen, at a long table, like a buffet.

I don't know why the Baroness thought I needed special protection, but she'd arranged with the local police station to have a 'police presence'. This took the form of a policewoman in a white van, who arrived just after lunch and said, 'Oh, Mrs Scott? You are to come with me.'

I'm just putting my bum on the seat of her van when her ladyship says, 'What are you doing in there?'

I said, 'Well . . .'

'I've asked her to come,' says the policewoman.

'Well, she's not coming with you, she's coming with me. Come along with me in my car.'

She took me to see an ancient chapel near her house, Maesyronen Chapel, the oldest nonconformist place of worship in Wales, and she told me that Oliver Cromwell once preached there. We got there and went inside and she said, 'You see, they've ruined it. *Ruined* it, Thora.'

It looked absolutely beautiful to me, very simple, almost like wattle and daub, and full of history. I said, 'Well . . . how? What's the matter with it?'

'It was entirely candle-lit before. Now look – they've put in electricity. Electric lights spoil everything.'

The Baroness is the daughter of a very strict Welsh priest. She has remained the way she was brought up – fiercely opposed to all alcoholic drinks, smoking and swearing. She said to Sue, who likes a ciggie, 'You can't smoke in the house . . . or in the garden.'

Sue said, 'Well, I can't very well go and sit in a field to smoke.'

So she and another sinner from the church found a hiding-place behind a monkey-puzzle tree in the garden and lit up. It was like being naughty at school. I said, 'I'll keep cave for you.'

I saw the Baroness approaching from the house, so I went to meet her and said, 'Oh, please show me your vegetable garden. I'd love to see the dahlias.'

It was perfectly true. I love to be shown the vegetable garden in these beautiful homes, because they are always in a walled garden. Her walls were of beautiful stone, and one had been broken down a bit, so she'd had it matched, which would cost a fortune I should think. It was all beautiful.

When we were having tea, all sitting at little tables, one table had two postcard-sized photographs on them, one of a woman and one of a man. A high court judge said to the Baroness, 'That's your brother Bert, isn't it?'

'Long time ago, of course. He's dead now.'

'And that's you there, when you were young?'

She suddenly seemed very put out. 'We know that. We don't need you sitting there telling us who it is. It's me.' And she turned them both face down. The whole day was like being in a comedy-mystery play.

Then she said to me, 'Come on, I want you to come along with me.' She took me into another room, medium-sized, with a rather nice royal blue carpet, quite plain. She said, 'I just wanted to show you – you see, you've got to be so careful in business . . . How do you like the carpet?'

I said, 'Well, I do.'

She said, 'My flat in London, near the church, I've been having it recarpeted, and I saw the fellow who had been doing it, going out with a roll of it. So I said to him, "Just come here, will you?"

'He came back and I said, "What have you got there?"

'He said, "Well, this is more than we want. There's too much."

'"And what are you going to do with that then? Use it in your house?"

'"Well, no, I . . . I thought, I . . . I just . . ."

'(He did not know what to say, Thora!) I said, "Well, you can just put it back."

'And look, Thora – it's done this room!'

April 1999

Marching as to York

Last spring, we all went by train to York, twenty of us, including the Baroness, the high court judge and another barrister who had a navy-blue bow tie with white spots, which he had tied himself, just like Scottie always did. None of your clip-ons. I said to him, 'I love you.'

We were going to York to see the Minster and to have

lunch with the Archbishop. There's a big room in the palace with a long table that seats twenty-four. It was himself, David Hope, the Archbishop, pouring out the tea for us all. That's what I love about him. He may be the second highest cleric in the land, a member of the House of Lords and live in a palace, but he never puts on airs and graces. I remember when I first met him on *Praise Be!* several years ago. He didn't live in a palace then; even though he was the Bishop of London he lived in a flat, and he made our tea himself. I inspected the china – which was rather good – while he was busy in the kitchen.

When he saw us off from York, some people from the press turned up and wanted a photograph of him and me with our arms round each other. I said, 'People will think we've just got married!'

He did me the greatest honour, this kind, handsome man, the Archbishop of York, when he came on as the surprise last guest for me on *This is Your Life* in 1997. He made time in his horribly busy schedule to travel all the way down from York to be on the programme. He only just made it in time, but what a joyful surprise for me to suddenly see him there. And then, after he'd said something nice about me, we were doing the walk-down at the end, and who should appear behind us but a Salvation Army Band – playing and singing 'O happy day' and 'Onward Christian soldiers'.

February 1999

24 February Daily Express *National Treasures lunch*

The *Daily Express* gives luncheons with everyone seated at the one table – it's the biggest table you've ever seen. I've been to quite a few – one I went to last February was because I had been voted by the readers of the *Express* a 'National Treasure', which is not quite how I think of myself, but still. They gave me a lovely lunch at the top of their building by the Thames, Number 1, Holborn, I think it is. It's a room with a miraculous view.

For all his 'loony left' leanings, I found Ken Livingstone to be very charming. He was certainly very nice to me, although I don't know why he wouldn't be. I had just met him at the 'Oldie' luncheon, and now here he was again two weeks later at this National Treasures lunch. We both arrived at the building at the same time and Ken grabbed my shopping bag and coat and helped me into the lift to the ninth floor. It was the day after Jeffrey Archer had announced that 'if I'm elected Mayor of London, I will give free milk to all schoolchildren'.

'I do wish I'd thought of that', sighed Ken, with a glint in his eye.

Jan and I had met Jeffrey Archer earlier in the year, at a 'Baby Lifeline' lunch in the Savoy for the Supermums Award. Jeffrey had told us how in the early sixties he had been a student working in his vacation on the promenade at Weston-super-Mare collecting deckchairs. He had heard that the film star Janette Scott was coming to the town, and had spent the day trying to get a glimpse of her because she was his pin-up.

Eventually he came upon Jan walking along the promenade . . . hand in hand with David Frost. (Jan and David were 'courting' for a while in the sixties.) Jeffrey told us that he had been so transfixed by the sight of Jan that he'd followed them for miles – until he'd suddenly remembered his deckchairs. He went flying back but arrived too late. His boss was there, and gave him his cards. 'Only the first', he told us, 'of many disasters!'

At the *Daily Express* lunch that day in February I was able to tell Lady Antonia Fraser that Jan and I had met her father, Lord Longford, at the Oldies luncheon. There had been a story in the papers that day that someone in America had plagiarised huge chunks of one of Antonia's books – the one about the gunpowder plot. Now I wonder, would anyone want to plagiarise my books?

October 1999

19 October Daily Express *luncheon*

On this latest occasion at the *Express* building I arrived
and I was sitting in the window looking out at the
amazing view again, and I saw Larry Adler come in. I
heard him saying to somebody, 'I'll be the oldest here
today.'

I said, 'Mr Adler, mind your words. How old are
you?'

He said, 'Eighty-three.'

I said, 'Eighty-eight.'

So I won that competition. Then it was a bit beautiful,
because during the speeches somebody called out to me
about *Praise Be!* They said, 'You don't do your hymn
programme any more, do you?'

I said, 'No, no, I did it for seventeen years, but it's ten
years since I last did it.'

'What a shame,' everyone said.

I'm always glad that people remember it with as much
affection as I do.

Then someone said, 'You've a favourite hymn, haven't
you?'

I said, 'Yes, of course, "Onward Christian soldiers".'

They said, 'Can you manage that, Larry?'

I thought, 'Oh, what a thing . . .'

Larry Adler played it beautifully, on the mouth-organ,
and in the end we were all singing it. It was really

something to see, in the middle of lunch, all those hardnosed journalists and me singing 'Onward Christian soldiers, marching as to war . . .'

I'm not ready to go yet, but I think it would be a good one for a funeral – with those words, 'Brothers we are treading where the saints have trod'. That and 'O happy day' will do me – eventually.

Northerners

July 1998

20–24 July Acton Rehearse Victoria Wood's Dinnerladies

Victoria Wood said the other day, 'In 1984 I tried to get our dear Thora for a show of mine – and she wasn't free until '89. And then I tried again in '89 and found that I'd missed by a day or two and it would be '91. But now I've had the joy of working with her.'

She's a lovely person. And working with her has been a great joy for me, too. Recently I had a little cameo role in her situation comedy *Dinnerladies*. There was Eric Sykes, Dora Bryan and me brought on as parents of the regular ones. We had a wonderful time. We had about five lines each, and my first line as I came on was looking at Celia Imrie and saying, 'Did you get that skirt from a catalogue?'

She said, 'No.'

I said, 'A pity. You could have sent it back.'

Dora Bryan was wearing a track suit. She went to wardrobe and they said, 'Will you look through those hats – to find a cap.'

She chose a mauve one that I'd just worn in *Last of the Summer Wine*. She came down on the set, and I said,

'You've got my bloody hat on.'

She said, 'Yes, I know, but you're not wearing it again, because they've told me so.'

So I had to take her word for that.

Jan said to me, 'I've worked with Eric, Mummy. He'll never do it twice alike.'

Someone had to say, 'What do you think of the cordless kettle?'

Eric was just drinking some tea, and his line was, 'I was a Desert Rat, and after shaving in sand and drinking muck, you can keep your cordless kettles.' Or words to that effect. He never said it twice alike. He used different expressions every time – only however he said it, it was always funny. Victoria didn't know where she was with him.

'Have you finished?' she said. Eric looked innocent. Anyway, I think she's having us all again.

The funny thing is that when I first started in the business, it was quite a handicap being northern. You tried not to let on too much, especially if you were in the London theatre. It was all right at Blackpool. I was in good company there, with Ken Dodd, Morecambe and Wise, Jimmy James, Arthur Askey and all of them. We were all northern comedy actors. But I hardly ever played 'northern' in the West End. You had to be either Cockney, or 'King's' English. Hardly anybody acted with a regional accent.

It only changed in the late fifties and sixties, with

plays like John Osborne's *Look Back in Anger* and all the angry young men writing for the theatre. Albert Finney and Tom Courtenay were the big young stars, and ever since then being northern has been rather an advantage, even in the legitimate theatre. In comedy, of course, there's never been a shortage of northern comics.

One of the best comedy writers to come out of the north in recent times is Victoria Wood. I love working with her. She's a good actress as well as a writer. And you know just how far to go with her stuff. And if you don't, you can say to her, 'Is that going too far?' and she'll say, 'No, it's fine' or 'Yes it is. Bring it down a bit.' I like that way of working – when the writer or director knows exactly what they want. She's very clever.

I was in *Pat and Margaret*, a play she wrote for television a few years ago. I played a rather possessive and tyrannical mother; I liked best a line I had about my son, when I'm telling a visitor, played by Celia Imrie, that my son's a bit backward.

'Only we didn't call it dyslexia then. You just sat at the back and did raffia.'

Duncan Preston was the son in that – another very good actor from the north. We had a good time, making it. I nearly finished him off on one shot that we did. I had to come to the telephone at the bottom of the stairs on the wall, and as I put it back on again, his line was, 'Was that Margaret?'

Mine was, 'No, it was your Auntie Rene. She wants you to get some more of that wool. Hey! Your ticket's hanging out.' (Meaning the label on his vest.)

I overheard the cameraman say to Gavin Millar, the director, 'Before you lose this set, I want to shoot loose on this wall.' (I won't explain it to you. I don't even know myself. It's just something they do.)

I said, 'Will there be sound?'

He said, 'No, it's just on the wall.'

I said, 'Don't tell Duncan there's no sound.'

So Gavin says, 'Right, we're going again, Duncan. Are you right?'

So he says his line, 'Was that Margaret?'

'No, it was your auntie. She wants you to get her some more of that wool. And hey – your flies are open!'

Duncan's jaw fell open and he sat there sort of stuttering. Then he said, 'Oh, have I spoiled the shot?'

I said, 'No, it's for Christmas cards for me.'

Speaker's Corner

November 1997, 1998, 1999

Queen's Speech – Opening of Parliament

The Speaker
requests the pleasure of the company of
Dame Thora Hird DBE
In the State Rooms, Speaker's House
following the State Opening of Parliament
12 until 1.00 p.m.
(Please bring this invitation with you)

A very dear friend of recent years is Betty Boothroyd, MP, better known by her official title of Madam Speaker. I love to watch *Westminster Live* on TV in the afternoon if I'm at home, just to see Betty saying 'Order! Order!' while some of our elected representatives in the House of Commons whoop and bang about like badly-brought-up children. How she manages to keep control of all of them *and* keep her temper is a wonder. I'd like to bang their heads together.

I first met Betty when she invited me for coffee soon after she was made Speaker, I think just because I was in show business and she wanted to meet me. We hit it off immediately. The next time she invited Jan as well. The Speaker's house, her home, is like a castle.

Now the nice thing is that she usually has a coffee morning on the day of the Queen's Speech, and then at about midday there's a big reception in the state rooms known as Speaker's Hall, which is gorgeous. About three hundred people come along, friends of the Speaker, Members of Parliament and their families, including the Prime Minister, and there's a champagne buffet lunch.

The first time I went with Jan to the Speaker's reception on the day of the Queen's speech, we took a taxi. We got to the end of Park Lane and there was a row of policemen in yellow coats.

'Sorry. You can't come through here today.'

From the moment the Queen leaves Buckingham Palace to go to the Houses of Parliament until the time that she returns home after making her speech, the roads between are closed to normal traffic. The streets are lined with people who come out to see the Queen. Every way we tried to go in this taxi a policeman barred our way.

'Sorry!'

And there was Jan with the big invitation card which they tell you to bring with you, which she kept showing to them and saying, 'Look! We're not *spies*, we're *guests*.'

But it was no good. In the end they made us go all the way down to the River Thames. When we got on the

Embankment a policeman told the driver, 'You'll have to go over Lambeth Bridge and back over Westminster Bridge.'

He said, 'Lambeth Bridge! But that'll take another twenty minutes.'

They said, 'It's the only way.'

Well, I tell you, in the end it cost me £23.50 for the taxi to get there.

These days, realising that it's a bit difficult for me getting through the crowds waiting for the royal procession, Betty now invites us to come early, while she is still getting herself dressed and ready for her big moment. This is always the best fun of the day, the time in her rooms before the opening ceremony and the official reception. As you may know, Betty was in show business before she became an MP. I believe she was a Tiller Girl. Apart from being a high kicker with great legs, she was in all sorts of theatrical productions, including pantomime, and when she is getting dressed in her magnificent Speaker's robes there is point in the procedure when she looks exactly like a principal boy. I told her, and in the blink of an eye, off she goes quoting from *Babes in the Wood*. She played all the roles, word perfect, and had us in stitches. We all get on very well, and we usually laugh all the way through. Then she goes into the chamber, looking very grand and formal, dressed in her gorgeous robes, and we sit and watch her proudly on the television in her room.

I remember when Patricia Routledge came to one of

the Speaker's coffee mornings. It happened to be on the same day that the late Princess Diana – who was a love – was going to be on television that evening, doing her 'tell all' interview with Martin Bashir. Pat was sitting there, having her coffee, alongside the Marchioness of Do-da, loveliest tartan suit you've ever seen, bit of velvet on the collar, and Lady Rhubarb in a pink hat . . . and so on. There were about eight of us, including the Speaker. And of course we were all talking about 'the dear gel':

'It will be so interestin' to hear what she has to say, d'you see . . . because I feel so *sorry* for the dear gel, d'you see.'

To which Miss Routledge says, 'Well, do you know what I would say to her? I should walk straight up and say, "Take that!", and she clapped her hand as though she were giving Princess Diana's face a good slap. There isn't a hush at the Cenotaph like there was in that room. We all sat there, playing statues.

I said, 'Well, it's a very strange thing you say, Pat. Would you like to know what I would do? I'd come up to you and say, "And you – take that!"' And I clapped my hands like she had done – only harder.

'Oh, I say! Bravo!' exclaimed all these upper-class voices, and I got a heartfelt round of applause.

I remember the Speaker's reception in November 1997. My arthritis had been acting up a bit, so Jan insisted that I go in my wheelchair, something I hate doing. But on this particular occasion it was so bad that I agreed. It was the first day of the 'New Labour' government, and Tony and Cherie Blair were doing their walkabout, hand in hand through the streets from Number Ten to the Houses of Parliament.

In the state room there was a little group of us, about three women and two men, all talking away, and a step away, in another group, I could see this little dark thing who kept looking at me and smiling and waving. Eventually she came over and said, 'I feel you're one of the family, because we've all known you so long!' Cherie Blair it was, but I didn't know this then. She knelt down next to my wheelchair and introduced herself. Since this was 'her' day, the first day of her husband's party being in power, I felt very flattered to be singled out. I offered her my congratulations, and she said it was such a thrill to meet me since, 'You have been part of everyone's life – for ever!' It made me feel a bit like Methuselah, but you have to expect that sort of thing when you reach my age.

2 December 1998 Michael Howard, coffee 10.30 a.m.

In 1998, because I'd had my fall in October, although I was home, I couldn't go to the Speaker's coffee morning. Jan went without me, and at the reception she found herself talking to Michael Howard, who was then the Shadow Home Secretary. He said to her, 'How's your mother?' As though he'd known me all his life.

We had met just once, going up in the lift at Broadcasting House, when he was the real Home Secretary. He and four men rushed into the lift just after I had got in and the doors were closing. He stood leaning against the wall with his papers in his hands and said, 'Hello!'

I said, 'Hello. By God, you only just caught that train!'

He said, 'How's your beautiful daughter?'

I said, 'Very well, thank you.' And they all got out at the next floor. That was all we said.

He came over to Jan at the Speaker's reception and asked after me, and Jan said, 'She's been in hospital, so she wasn't up to coming today.'

He said, 'Would it be wrong of me to ask for her telephone number and address?' She said it wouldn't be wrong at all and gave it to him, and a few days later he came round to see me at home, with a big box of really good chocolates.

I said, 'Well, it's very nice to see you . . . and your chocolates. You won't have to talk politics to me.'

He said, 'That makes a nice change.'

We had coffee and chatted away like old pals. Nothing of the night about him at all. More like a nice, polite schoolboy who was surprised to have come top of the class. He's also a very proud family man. He's got a son who is a devout Christian and a daughter who had just got a triple first at Cambridge. We had a delightful chat.

After nearly three-quarters of an hour he said, 'You must excuse me now, but I've a meeting at twelve.'

I said, 'Is it something important at the House?'

He said it was, so I said, 'Oh well, I'll let you go then. Have I to get you a taxi?'

He said, 'No, I've kept the car.' And sure enough, there in the mews was his car and chauffeur and detective and all of that, standing outside my front door waiting for him.

I said, 'That's all at our expense, you know that, don't you?'

I do see life, don't I? But what a nice fellow. He can come and see me again with a box of chocolates any time he likes.

As I write this, my invitation from the Speaker for the State Opening of Parliament in November 1999 is sitting on my mantelpiece. Next to it is my invitation to a millennium breakfast on the same morning, at the East India Club, St James's Square, where I will be one of three guest speakers. The other two are the film director David Puttnam, now Lord Puttnam of Queen's Gate, and my dear friend David Hope, Archbishop of York. And next to those two invitations – guess what? No, you can't guess, so I'll tell you: aeroplane tickets for Jan and me to fly to New York on 20 November. I'll tell you the reason for that in the next chapter.

Lost for Words

November 1999

So many nice things have been happening to me lately. I sometimes think people are going to be ready to shoot me if I get anything else. I really have been so lucky in my life. Jan and I flew to New York in November because *Lost for Words* had been short-listed for an International Emmy – the Best Drama Award. That's one of the top American television awards, and, like the BAFTA over here, is a great prize. Everyone involved in the production is honoured by it – the writer, the director and the actors.

It all started at the Huddersfield Hotel. I think it must have been in the summer of 1986, or perhaps it was 1985. I can't remember. Anyway, we were up in Yorkshire filming *Last of the Summer Wine*. (I always stay at the Huddersfield Hotel when I'm there. Fourteen of us do. Two-star. I was sitting outside one evening. They have a few tables and chairs at the end of the street – don't imagine it is Las Vegas or anything. One day the sun must have come out, and quick, they were off, 'Come on! Let's buy twenty tables, Joe! Go on, and chairs enough for round 'em.')

So I was sitting there at the end of the day's work in the evening sun. It was nearly dinner time, and the waiter said, 'You're wanted on the phone.' It was Derek Longden.

Now I didn't know him very well, except I'd been in a television play a few years ago, screenplay by Jack Rosenthal, of a book that Derek had written about his first wife, Diana. The play was called *Wide-eyed and Legless*, with Julie Walters as Diana, and Jim Broadbent as Derek. It was a story about a wife who develops ME and her husband who cares for her, and in it I'd played Derek's mother who was beginning to go senile. In the end the wife dies. It was a sad story, very poignant, and when I first read the script I thought it was strange having it played by three comedy actors. But then I saw why – because the way that Derek Longden gets through the sadness of life is by keeping his sense of humour alive. There were some very funny moments in the play. It was autobiographical – he writes about true things – and while we were shooting it he would kneel down at my side and say, 'Ye gods, you do remind me of my mother.'

On the telephone that evening in Huddersfield he was saying, 'I've written a book about my mother that follows on from the last one, about her last years. Can I come and show you?'

I said, 'Well, where are you? Where are you ringing from?'

He said, 'I live only five minutes from your hotel.'

So he came over and had dinner with me that night. He had a copy of his book about his mother, and there was a picture of me on the front cover, from when I was playing his mother in *Wide-eyed*.

I said to him, 'I hope Felix de Wolfe doesn't see that picture. Or you're going to be sorry you didn't ask my permission for it in the first place.'

Anyway, he tells me he wants to write a television film about his mother, based on this book he's written. So he's having his dinner with me, as my guest, and he's saying, 'Would you like another glass of wine?'

'Yes. Well, come on, say what you want to say.'

He said, 'Well, the first thing to say is, I'm not going to do it if you are not interested – but I'm going to try to get some backing from America.'

A lot of people may not realise that these days most major television plays are given financial backing by individuals and companies with spare money. All the money for a production doesn't come from the BBC or ITV. 'Angels' we call them in the theatre.

I said, 'Give over lying, Derek.'

'How do you mean?'

I said, 'You know damn well that if I'm not interested, you'll still sell it for somebody else. And you should. But when you try and sell it, I don't want you to mention me. Don't mention my name in connection with it. Let's just see how things go.'

Two weeks later he comes back to the hotel with his

wife, Aileen, so I have them to dinner again. I'm still there for the filming of *Last of the Summer Wine*. Aileen is his second wife, who is blind, whom he had married after his first wife had died of the ME. She came into the first play, too.

Aileen says, 'Isn't it nice he's going to write a play about you?'

I said, 'Not until I see what he's doing, he's not.'

She laughed and turned to him, 'Isn't it like her, this? It's like your mother!'

About a year later I was back in Huddersfield again, and he came round to see me. I said, 'Did anything happen?'

He said, 'Oh, yes.' He could hardly wait to tell me. Apparently after he'd been to see me a woman in America, half Red Indian, who was one of a group of backers who had bought and financed *Wide-eyed and Legless*, had written to him and said, 'What are you doing at the moment?'

He had written back and told her he was writing this play about his mother, and she had asked to see it. He said to me, 'I promise you, on my honour, I never mentioned you. I sent her the play, about 80 per cent complete, and I never mentioned your name.'

I said, 'No, well, I'm glad you didn't.'

Then he showed me the letter that had come back: 'If you can get Thora Hird interested, we'll buy it.'

He left me with a copy of the play, not quite complete, but nearly. I took it to my caravan on the lot. I must say,

I was having a little weep as I was reading it. Kathy Staff came in. 'What's the matter?'

I said, 'It's nothing. I'm reading a script, and it just upset me a little bit.'

'Well, put it away. You don't want upsetting like that.' She's always like that, Kathy. She tries to protect me.

I liked the play. I suppose any actress would say this – I knew what I could do with the part. I liked the way he wrote about things, like all her little bits of china. She'd see a bit of china, and buy it. It would get knocked on the side of the sink, and its head would come off. Next time Derek saw it, it would be stuck on some other bit of china with a bit of match stick holding it together, and it could be a dog's head on a woman's body, or a cat could end up wearing a crinoline.

There were a lot of lines that I thought were worth saying. Like, 'I'm only just beginning to be glad he's dead.' Or when she passes a woman being wheeled along in the hospital who mouths to her the name of what she's got, some terrible illness, she turns to her son and says, 'She must be French, with a name like that.'

And I loved the line about the Chinese couple in the chip shop. 'They've got a lovely little baby . . . He's Chinese as well.'

You know, people do say these things. He writes about true things.

25 March–17 April Lost for Words *Leeds*

So that was the play, *Lost for Words*. The mother has three strokes in it, and then she dies. Derek said, 'I know your husband died of a stroke, and I wouldn't want to upset you, but you'll know what it means.'

When I knew the play was written for me, and I knew how much it was written for me, I said, 'I'd like Alan Bell to direct this.'

It's lovely to be able to talk to your director, and Alan's someone like that for me. He has been directing me in *Last of the Summer Wine* for years, and I like the way he works, because he came up in the business through being a film editor. They nearly always make good directors. But as it happens he had told me, just in passing – not meaning anything – that he had never directed a single television play. We work well together, and he's been very good to me, so I said I wanted him to direct this one.

They said, 'Have you any reason for that?'

'Yes, because he understands me.' So they had to agree.

Alan and I travelled up together by train. We were doing it in Leeds, and I was so looking forward to working in the studios again, because I'd had so many happy years there, working on *In Loving Memory*. The meeting place in the restaurant had been marvellous . . . but it's all gone. Everything's different. Things do have to change, I know, but it was a bit sad. Just a few old faces to talk about the old days with. All the crew and people working in props, make-up and wardrobe were wonderful to me.

The first read-through – when the entire cast come together to read the play all the way through – was like a production of the *Messiah*. There were so many people that had words, like all the people that came to the door to see round her house when she's selling it. And they'd nearly all worked with me before, so it was like a grand reunion.

I had a double, and she brought me some ten by eight photographs to show me what she used to do. She was a stripper. There she was, standing with nothing on, completely starkers, with just her hands in front of her fanny.

'Oh, yes!' I said. 'Well, I'll tell you something – I could never have understudied you!'

There were about seven people who had put money in it. The original woman, who Derek had told me about, took me to lunch and said how much they had hoped I would be in it, and how glad they were that I was in it. She was very nice, and they were all very nice to me. But I'll tell you what was odd – I've never known a bunch of people stand on a set watching you shoot, just because they had money in it. Our form in England is for the producer and backers not to come on the set. They look at the rushes the next day, or at the end of day, to see what has been shot. But these people stood and watched every scene as we shot it. Not out of selfishness, but it made life a bit difficult for Alan. They spent much more money than they needed have done, with all the things they wanted him to retake.

There are very long corridors at Leeds, and my arthritis played me up quite a bit. When you're in pain a lot of the time you are not going to tell anybody, but it is tiring. I always knew I'd be able to cope with the help of God. I had a lot of pain when I was in Leeds, but I'd go to bed at night and in two minutes I was off. I was up again at half past five every morning. I was all right, because I had the car to and from the studio each day.

It came out very close to the Alan Bennett play, also about an old lady, so I had to make the two parts different. The thin line I had to walk down, in my own mind, was that Violet, the old lady of ninety-four in Alan Bennett's play, was not mental. She was old, but she was all there. Whereas the mother in *Lost for Words* was only about seventy-eight, so she was quite active, at least at the beginning, but a little bit distracted in the head. Like showing her cat the receipt for the carpet, when it was scratching it up. This always used to happen, apparently, when Derek was telephoning her. He used to ring her every morning, like Jan rings me, to see she was alive.

So it was: 'Hello. Yes, love, I'm all right. Eh, eh, Whiskey! Come off that carpet. You what? Yes, he's at the carpet again. Whiskey! Do you know how much that carpet cost? Look, I'll show you how much it was . . .'

and off she goes upstairs to get the bill to show the bloody cat what the carpet had cost, while Derek's left dangling on the end of the telephone.

We did that scene in *Wide-eyed*. We had another scene with the cat in *Lost for Words*, where she's giving it a bath. The joy was that the cat we used liked being bathed. There was no scratching. And the woman who owned it was there all the time, because it was a precious cat. She used to say to him, 'Oh! You have done well! Now Thora will tell you how well you did. You are such a little star.'

Well, he was very good, but I said to her, 'Be careful what you tell him. He'll be wanting top billing next.' He wouldn't have been the only one, either.

Postscript 24 November 1999

Returned from New York. Yes! We won!

The whole trip was huge fun. Jan came with me, and the first wonderful thing to happen was that Virgin upgraded our seats to first-class. Talk about travelling in style! It was fantastic. You could order your meal whenever you wanted it, and anything you wanted, and all of it delicious. No sitting waiting patiently for a trolley and then being handed a plate of plastic bags you can't open and food that has been selected for you. They even had a masseuse aboard. I had my legs and feet done, and Jan had a back massage, and then they gave us lovely duvets to cuddle up in for a nap.

We were staying, courtesy of Yorkshire Television, at

the Hilton Hotel, where among the other guests were 1,500 cheer leaders, all prancing around in their little costumes, who had come to practise for the great Thanksgiving Day Parade. Everywhere you went there were these little girls darting about, all smiling and charming and with every kind of accent from all the different parts of America. It was all so typically American, it felt like being in a film.

One day Jan wheeled me out in my chair for a personal grand tour of New York. We saw the skaters on the outside rink at the Rockefeller Plaza; Radio City; St Patrick's Roman Catholic Cathedral where the nobs like the Kennedy family are all married; then we went along Fifth Avenue singing all the songs with Fifth Avenue in them that we could think of. We had our lunch in Trump Tower, which has an amazing inside waterfall that comes down from the top of the sky-scraper to the basement, where we were sitting, down a mile-high, pink, marble wall. We went into Central Park and along the Avenue of the Americas, where Jan pointed out her bank, as though it were one of the sights. By the time we were back in our twenty-sixth-floor apartment, three hours later, poor Jan was nearly dropping with exhaustion.

The Emmy Award ceremony was another wonderful affair. It began with a reception in the Penthouse suite, on the forty-fourth floor of the Hilton. The view from there across Manhattan by night was staggering. Alan Bell and his wife Constance were there with us,

Derek and Aileen Longden, and Keith Richardson, the Controller of Yorkshire Television. The barrister, Clive Anderson, was the Master of Ceremonies. He told me the next morning that his wife had sent him over with a huge shopping list to get all the presents for their children for Christmas.

Like all these prize-giving ceremonies, it went on forever – five hours – which always makes it rather an ordeal. Our production, *Lost for Words*, was in the last category, because it was the main one of the evening, the Emmy for the Best International Drama. There had been 700 entries originally, with a large number coming from Japan. This was whittled down to forty-five; and then we were in the final short list of three, with an Italian detective drama, and a very intriguing Japanese drama which Jan said she would have very much liked to have seen more of. They only showed us a little bit of each one, of course, including ours.

And when he announced the winner of the Best International Drama – we had won! Derek and Alan wheeled me up onto the stage to receive it on behalf of the whole team, and you should have heard the cheers. Jan said that it was almost like being at Lourdes, because I had nearly flown up onto the stage in my chair, but when we reached the platform, I stood up and walked across to Clive Anderson. In my speech I said that no ship can sail without a good captain and crew, and that we had been so lucky to have Alan Bell as our director, Derek to write such beautiful words, and Yorkshire

Television to have the faith in us to put it on. So it was all a great experience.

I've had so many wonderful letters from people congratulating me, including one from Tony Blair, and a separate one from Cherie Blair. Isn't it strange how it's so often very busy people, like Prime Ministers and barristers, who will take the time and trouble to write kind letters? The Emmy is a gold female figure carrying a globe over her head, and it's for all of us, the writer, director and cast. They said that I should keep it in my home . . . so that's all to be polished and dusted, you know.

Awards and tributes

June 1999

*25 June Tribute Lunch for Judith Chalmers OBE,
Dorchester Hotel*

This lunch in June 1999 – you've never seen anything
like it. It's a bit difficult to tell it, myself, because it
sounds like bragging.

Judith Chalmers is President of the Lady Taverners,
who raise money for charity. They are the female branch
of the cricketing lot, the Lord's Taverners. Judith and
her wonderful sister Sandy, who works every hour God
sends for Help the Aged and Age for Stage, are part of
my closest circle of friends, the people I'm most fond
of.

To explain about this tribute lunch, this is the letter I
received from the secretary of the Lady Taverners:

Dear Dame Thora,
You very kindly attended our tribute lunch for Judith
Chalmers at the Dorchester Hotel in 1997. It really
was a super occasion, a complete sell-out. We had
eight speakers who were limited to two minutes each.
There was a short auction of three lots, and the event

was thoroughly enjoyable. It raised over £30,000, and if I may say so, it was in a different mould from other tribute lunches.

The Council decided to make this an annual event to be called 'The Judith Chalmers Tribute Lunch to *Name of person to be honoured*'. Judith has been asked to nominate different people each year, and to host the proceedings. Last year we honoured June Whitfield.

Judy, with the full backing of the Lady Taverners' Council, would be delighted if you would agree to be our guest of honour for this year's Tribute Lunch. If you are agreeable, we would like to hold the event on Friday 25 June. It would be lots of fun. Please give me a ring if you would like to discuss this further or alternatively you can speak to Judy or Sandy.

Right. Well, of course I was agreeable. Jan and her husband William came with me to the Dorchester. On my table I had Jan and William, Alan Bell and his wife and Michael Parkinson and his wife. Judith was the President so she was on my left and her husband, Neil, on my right. He and I have a joke that goes on forever, because I never get his name right – people's names are becoming increasingly a problem for me – and I call him all sorts. When I write to Judith I always put, 'Give my love to Moses' and she'll put in her reply 'Love from Ezekiel' or something equally daft.

The whole place was packed with invited people,

who had all bought tickets. Victoria Wood came, Roger Royle, Eric Morecambe's widow, Joan, Eric Sykes, Nicholas Parsons, Sherrie Hewson – I can't think of all the names now of everyone there, but it was all very loving.

They served the luncheon, and after the first course three people spoke. And then after the next course three more people said something, all limited to two minutes each.

All sorts of different people spoke. Judith Chalmers, as the President, spoke first, then Michael Parkinson, Nicholas Parsons, Norman Wisdom, Keith Barron – you never heard such flattery as Keith Barron's words.

'And what is more, any of you who have ever worked with her don't need me to tell you, you already know that she is the greatest actress this country has produced!'

Norman Wisdom presented me with a beautiful bouquet.

Norman reminded me of the time the two of us were trying to stop smoking. We were doing – I could have told you the name of the film just now. It was a Rank comedy, one of a series of very funny films he made in the fifties, and in it I was the cook, and Norman was the boot boy. I had been trying to give up smoking for a while, because in those days everyone was just catching on to the idea that there might be a health risk, and one morning in the make-up room, Norman asked me to help him give up too.

I said, 'I'll tell you what, you've a journey to get here in the morning. So have I. Let us promise each other – look at me now, look at me – promise me that you won't have one before you get here, in the make-up room. Even if you have one then.'

'All right.'

So the following morning he's all bright and cheerful, 'I've not had a cigarette. Can I have one now?'

I said, 'No. I'll tell you what we'll do. Let's not have one until we go to rushes at one o'clock.' (Rushes – that's looking at the previous day's work that you've filmed.) I said, 'When you come out of rushes, you can have one then.' Which is what happened.

So we were both doing very well. Several days go by, and then one day when he kisses me good morning I say, 'Look me in the eyes. Look at me. Have you had a cigarette?'

He said, 'No.'

I said, 'Well, what's that you've just breathed all over me? Scotch mist?'

I thought he needed a lesson. So I said to the prop man, 'Have you got a chocolate box in the prop room?'

He said, 'Yes. A big 'un.'

I said, 'Good. When they sweep up all the fag-ends off the floor at the end of the day, will you put them all in it and give it to me tomorrow? And can you make it look like a new box?'

As well as making the film, Norman was on at the London Palladium in the evenings, and I was at the Strand Theatre, doing *The Trouble Makers*. The car used to pick me up after the show at the Strand, then I'd go and pick him up at the Palladium, we'd get the late train down to Brighton together, and shared a taxi to The Mitre, where we were staying during the filming. They always left us our supper out, if you could call it supper – bits of cabbage curled up, bits of tomato, dried, just left over from when they'd had dinner. It's all glamour, you see, this acting life.

So the next morning, on the film set, the prop man handed me this box of chocolates, full of fag-ends. It looked like a beautiful four-pound box, all covered in cellophane paper. I got someone at the Palladium to put it into Norman's dressing-room.

On the way home he said, 'I was given a lovely box of chocolates from a fan.'

'How nice.'

'Oh, beautiful.'

The following day he comes up to me, 'Did you send me that horrible box of fag-ends?'

I said, 'Just a moment. Just a moment. Why would I send you fag-ends – you're a non-smoker, aren't you?'

It was tough love – but it cured him!

He loves anything sad, Norman. Comics often do. He said to me one day, 'We could do a wonderful film together. You could be my mother, and I'd be your son. But I'd have something wrong with me.' You get this with comics, you know. They love to play pathos. Norman does it very well, with that wistful little face of his.

I said, 'Oh, yes, that would be funny. I'm laughing now.'

'No. Wait. We're standing waiting for a bus. And there are people in front of us. And just when it gets to me getting on – the door closes in my face. Can't you see it? Everyone would go, "Ah!"'

I said, 'Not me. I wouldn't go "Ah" because I'd have missed the bus then.'

Whenever I see him, like at this lunch, he still says to me, 'We'll do that film one day!'

I say, 'What, the one with you and me waiting for the bus? I can't wait.'

Back at the luncheon – I had a wonderful surprise when Michael Parkinson presented me with the BAFTA statuette for the Alan Bennett play, that John Thaw had collected for me on the night of the official ceremony, because I'd had a cold and couldn't attend. Parky said I was a National Treasure, and should be made into a monument. And on my table there was another BAFTA – made in chocolate – which is in my fridge now. And you cannot tell which is the real one and which is chocolate.

There was even a message from the Queen. They'd invited her to the lunch, and of course she couldn't come, but they read out the beautiful letter she'd sent in reply. That's Her Majesty. There were other messages, poems and tributes from many good friends. Jan was one of the speakers during the meal. She said, 'There are just so many things you don't know about my mother . . .' She told them a few little things, and when she got to the end she said, 'And another thing you can't know – how wonderful it is for me that she's my mother.' I was sitting there feeling – ooh! I don't know if I deserve all this.

I cannot tell you how wonderful it was. At the end, the Salvation Army marched on, through all the tables, and up onto the stage, playing 'Onward Christian soldiers'. The Lady Taverners made £32,000 for charity, and for me it was the most unexpected and flattering and surprising day of my life, nearly.

The most flattering day of all was probably when I was made Queen of the May at school, when I was six. On the blackboard, for the voting, the teacher used to put in chalk:

> Not the wittiest one
> Nor the prettiest one
> Nor she with the gown most gay
> But she who is pleasantest all the day through
> With the kindest of things to say and to do
> She shall be Queen of the May.

We had a very big green cloth that was put down for the

barefoot dancing, in case there were any spills in the floor. I mean splinters. We would say, 'Ooh, I've got a spill in my finger.' Also if we were dancing at a garden party, this was put on the grass, because the grass could be wet, or have nettles. For the May Queen's coronation this covering was put over all the chairs and desks, piled up at the back of the school to make a throne, with me on the top. Only I fell off, didn't I? Royalty toppled. Dethroned, with my crown a crop of daisies. They picked me up and there were no bones broken. I tried not to cry, and I didn't very much.

22 January 1998
12 for 1 Melvyn Bragg South Bank Show *party, Savoy*

Just in case you think I only want to tell you about my winning awards, you might know that I hand over a few and all. Melvyn Bragg gave a luncheon at the Savoy in January, with lots of tables full of celebrity guests. Alan Bennett was at my table, and one away from me was Pat Routledge. Victoria Wood was at the next table but came over for a chat about *Dinnerladies*.

I had been invited to present an award, and it gave me particular pleasure this time, because Jenny Snape, my very dear dresser on *Last of the Summer Wine*, has a young son who is an actor. A film had come out that everybody was talking about – *The Full Monty* – about men strippers. Well, the lad in it, William Snape who played Nathan the young boy, was Jenny's son, and I was there to give him his award, which I did with great pleasure.

Talking about dressers, I will never forget Rose Neighbours. Rose was another wonderful dresser who worked with me for years. She had started working in a tea bar in Shepherd's Bush, and the stories she used to tell me . . . Then she'd moved on to Lower Regent Street, near the theatre. That was all before I knew her. Then she was twelve years as a dresser at the BBC but she had to retire at sixty. Unlike the theatre, where you can still be on the boards at ninety, at the BBC it's like being a civil servant. However good you are – out you go.

Rose dressed me both for *Meet the Wife* and for *First Lady*. Lillian, who was deaf, was Rose's assistant. For *First Lady* we had a thing like a telephone booth in the middle of the floor. While the cameras shot on black – David Proudfoot, the director, was a great one for running on black instead of cutting – Rose and Lillian could change me out of suit, shoes, gloves and earrings and into a ball-gown or whatever in thirty seconds flat. The two of them. As fast as I'm telling you. Nobody would be speaking. We always did it in front of a live audience, so the audience just waited silently while this was going on, and then I'd walk out of the booth again, dressed for the next scene. You need all these wonderful professionals to enable you to do this, you see.

Now – will you follow me, please? Have you got your ticket? Only ticket-holders come into the next room! I know this may sound like bragging, but I have been presented with four awards in twelve weeks, for being on time and knowing my words and that sort of thing. And all around my eighty-eighth birthday, so I hope I can be forgiven for wanting to show them to you.

Now, here we are, Ladies and Gentlemen. Here's the exhibition. (They all need polishing, you know.)

On your right, you have the Lifetime Achievement Award. Dame Thora Hird. Comedy Awards 1998.

The silver one over there is the Oldie of the Year 1998. Well, nobody wants to get that, because you've to be old enough.

Royal Television Society Programme Awards, Actor, Female for *Talking Heads*: 'Waiting for the Telegram'.

And here, in the centre, is my BAFTA for 'Waiting for the Telegram'. It's not squinting at me now – but it was.

Felix de Wolfe, my agent, came back to the mews with me after the Judith Chalmers Tribute Lunch, and he carried in the BAFTA for me. The real one, not the chocolate one. After he had gone, Nola, my companion, says, 'Look, somebody's dropped this. Look at it.'

It was looking at me squint-eyed and a bit quizzically. I said, 'It's looking at me as if to say, "I don't know if you deserve me!"'

The next day Felix telephoned and I asked him, 'Did you drop the BAFTA?'

'No! Of course I didn't.'

I said, 'Well, did your Caroline drop it?'

'No!'

'Did Alan Bell drop it? He said he didn't. Sandy said she didn't. Somebody's dropped it, because it's looking at me as if to say, "I don't know how you've got me!"'

So Felix says, 'Well, the reason I'm telephoning is to say that they're sending round for it, to have the thing with your name put on.'

I said, 'Well, will you please ask them to give me one that looks as though it thinks I deserve it?'

It really was looking at the other awards on the sideboard as if to say, 'What were you for?'

It's all right now – but who did drop it?

Stars and garters

November 1999

18 November Star and Garter bazaar

For many years now I've been going several times a year to visit the men at the Star and Garter Home for wounded ex-servicemen, in Richmond. They are the lads who gave their limbs for us in the war, who are now all elderly gentlemen. I've always had a weakness for the great war veterans. My great friend Dorothy Crisp is head welfare officer there. I've got to know a lot of the men over the years. I always go along whenever they have open days, special church services, and above all I like to visit them for their spring and autumn bazaars.

I think I first met them when I was filming for *Praise Be!* – the making of poppies for Remembrance Sunday by the British Legion, which is also based in Richmond. Some of the men from the Star and Garter who aren't too badly disabled help make the thousands and thousands of poppies.

Jimmy, one of the men that I got to know quite well, died last Christmas, just six days before his hundredth birthday. Many years ago he said to me, 'I right fancy you, you know.'

I said, 'Oh, do you, Jimmy? How nice. I wish you'd mentioned it before.'

One day he said to me, 'How old are you?'

I said, 'Eighty-three' – which I was then, when we had this conversation.

'Oh,' he said. 'Get off. Come back when you're a bit older!'

They all have jokes with me. They've a rare sense of humour. Dorothy, who is a wonderful woman, invented 'chair' dancing for them. The wives can come in every day, whenever they like, and they have evening parties. One of the men said to me, 'Thora, I am sorry I can't take you dancing tomorrow night.'

I said, 'Oh, can't you? How disappointing. There isn't anybody else, is there?'

He said, 'No, only the chiropodist is coming, and I don't want to miss him.' And he started laughing. This was a man with no legs.

I've got a sign written at the top of my stairs in the mews – everyone remarks on it – it says, 'I grumbled when I had no shoes – until I met a man that had no feet.' That's how I feel when I go to visit these men. How dare I complain about my aches and pains when I see what they have to put up with without complaining at all?

There was one the other day, good-looking, a really handsome fellow, who looked a bit young, I thought, to be in there. I asked Dorothy about him afterwards. She told me he'd been down under water inspecting a sunken ship for bombs or something, and something had gone wrong with his equipment, and he'd got the bends. Now he's paralysed. He can't move anything.

Dorothy knows all about them. I go to have coffee and biscuits with her and we sit with the men in the big room – the Queen's ballroom – where we can look out at the gardens, which are really beautiful. She even knows which man likes which kind of biscuit. She'll say, 'Don't take one of those, Eric. You won't like that kind. Have one of these.' She has so much love for them all.

The last time I called I met Sid Philips' brother. Now, in my opinion – I don't want to offend anyone, this is just what I think – nobody can play 'Happy days are here again' like the Sid Philips Band could, with Sid on the clarinet. I was in a play called *Happy Days* that had been written for me, which played twice nightly in Blackpool. When I gave the curtain speech, down on the apron, I'd get them to play the record and I used to tap-dance to it as I made my exit – just to prove to the audience I could do it. You should have heard the roar of applause that used to get.

If you ever go near Richmond, go and see them all at the Star and Garter. You won't regret it. The gardens alone are worth seeing, and the men love company. As you approach Richmond you see this lovely big building, with 'Star and Garter' written up.

March 1999

18 March Foresters' Charity Dinner 7.30 p.m.

The Ancient Order of Foresters made Jimmy and me
Foresters for life, and also John Tudor, our friend who
was minister at Westminster Methodist Central Hall
until 1998. Foresters are like masons. They do a lot for
charity that people don't know about.

Two summers ago they opened a beautiful summer
hut, a sunroom for elderly people, in Essex. They
dedicated it to Scottie, after he had died of a stroke.
They had windows that open inside it, so you can sit in
the fresh air but still be under the roof.

I love it when people show how much they loved
Scottie. I went to open the Stroke Association's new
building in Staffordshire, where he grew up, and there's
a plaque on the wall, all in wood, 'Opened by Thora
Hird, in memory of James Scott'.

April 1998

30 April Russian photographer coming

The Russian photographer – that was for a church that
wanted to raise money for an orphanage in Russia.
They wanted me to go over to Russia to be in a
documentary film visiting the orphans, and I said I

would do it – until Jan blew her stack.

She said, 'Russia! You? In your state of health? Visiting an orphanage where you'd have to be carried out even if you were well . . . Even I couldn't do it.'

So I couldn't do that. Jan says you have to be incredibly strong to do it, to be able detach yourself emotionally from these helpless little children. But the photographer did come and take my picture, and they used it on their brochures to help raise money.

I hope all this doesn't sound too goody-goody. I'm not at all, but anybody who has been as lucky as I have, and been given so much, wants to put a bit back. If you've become a bit known, there's a lot you can do if you put your mind to it.

I was down at Milton Keynes last summer, to open a church fete for Kathy Staff's daughter, Susan, who's a vicar there. Kathy took me down in the car. There were lots of people there and of course they immediately started to ask for our autographs. I said to Kathy, 'Eh-up. We can make a bob or two out of this.'

We sat at a little table, with a bowl, and charged 50p an autograph – two for the price of one. We made nearly £100 – not bad for an afternoon's work!

Huddersfield Market
(and more tales of
Last of the Summer Wine)

September 1999

20 September Last of the Summer Wine *audience showing*

In the old days of making *Last of the Summer Wine*, all the exteriors were done on film, but the indoor scenes were performed on a stage in front of an audience. Like you do a play. And so the laughter you heard was their laughter. Now they put the laughs in after. It's rather a shame. But it is still genuine laughter you hear, at the scenes we've performed. We go to a studio and the whole episode is shown to the audience, on a big screen, and their laughs are recorded.

Some of the cast go along to these showings and introduce them, and do a bit of a turn to 'warm the audience up'. I wasn't asked to go along to do this, and at first I thought it was because I didn't have a big enough part. I said to Alan Bell, 'Is it because my part isn't big enough?'

He said, 'Don't talk daft. You'd bring the roof down if you came. But I'm not going to ask you to do things like that.'

I said, 'Whyever not?'

He said, 'Because I'm not.'

Then he said, 'Well, would you like to come one Sunday?'

I said, 'Yes – and show you.'

'Wesley' was at one side of the stage and said something derogatory about me, Edie, and I was off-stage the other side. I shouted, 'I heard that!' and came on, and the roof came in.

I don't do gags like that now. The viewings are still something I like to go to, because you feel you get to know the audiences you are playing to. But now I just come on and sit on a chair for five minutes and talk about the making of it and our life on the gypsy encampment while we're doing the filming.

It is like a gypsy encampment. Behind the scenes are all our caravans where we sit in the sunshine talking and chatting, because sometimes we have to wait about for the weather. It's all miles out in the countryside. In midsummer it is really beautiful, because the heather is all coming out. With it all being hills, you need the summer light for filming.

Peter Sallis and Frank Thornton share a big caravan now, which I only know because I had to go in and use their loo the other day. We used to have our own smaller caravan and loo, for Kathy, Jane Freeman and me, but there's a new thing we have now, a room at the back of a truck. There's the truck in the front, and there's a small room at the back – but no toilet, just a wardrobe and a settee. Of course, they've got mobile lavatories on the lot – but we are never shooting anywhere near the encampment. Consequently, when we are filming, where do you go to pee? You spend a lot of time thinking about these things when you live a glamorous life like mine.

Sometimes I don't see the three men up there at all, even on the gypsy encampment. It's all done as separate comedy scenes, rather than as a narrative drama, and I'm usually involved with the ladies' coffee morning scenes. I've done a couple of scenes with 'Auntie Wainwright', but most years I don't come across Jean Alexander. She's often finished in the shop the day before we get up there.

Danny O'Dea, who plays Eli, comes for one day – and there's a laugh in everything he does. Walking into lampposts and taking off his hat to apologise. Talking to the dog, 'I'm sorry. How are you? How's your mother?'

Danny's my friend. He'll come in and he'll say, 'You haven't put that back bedroom up for me yet, have you?'

It's all pretend. If there are people watching us, which is very rare, because we're normally miles out in the country, he'll say, 'Have you got that fellow staying with you again? I've told you before, he'd better not be there when I get home. I'm sick of it! Sick to death of it.'

He's a lovely old love, and a real old pro. He's been in the business forever. I was giving him a lift home, because he lives nearby, and I said to him, 'You do remind me of a comedian that my husband used to play for in variety.'

He said, 'Who was that?'

I said, 'Archie Glen.'

'My uncle,' he said. 'It's a lot of his stuff I do.'

Archie Glen used to come on stage in an opera hat and dinner jacket, holding a newspaper of fish and chips, and he used to be funny with these chips, making out they were far too hot. Then he used to say, 'I'm going home. I'll get into trouble, because I'm not going home for last night . . . I'm going home for the night before.'

Eli only gets one line in some programmes, but he earns all his money with that one line, because he gets such a laugh with it.

I'm lucky if I get three lines. 'Drink your coffee.' I have to get a laugh out of that.

Bill – Compo – was always the leader of the three men. It was always him kicking the stones about and saying, 'Let's go down the pub.' Peter – Cleggy – more or less just says the words, but he has that lovely laconic voice that sounds just right. When I see Clegg sitting in his little house, I think, 'I'd love one of those.' There's a row of them, just like the one my Auntie Clara lived in. I love to see Clegg sitting there with his paper, and his cup of tea. You can see that he's made it himself, he sits like that every morning, and he always knows if it's Howard from next door.

All the houses we use in *Last of the Summer Wine* are

like the ones I remember as a child, two steps up from the road. There's one for sale next to the one that's supposed to be mine, and I look at this stone-fronted thing every time I'm there and think, 'I could buy it, and live there. On my own.' Of course I couldn't. But I like to imagine. It's just nostalgia.

Auntie Clara and Uncle Walter lived in a little row of houses in Walsden. They were both mill workers. White cotton sheets. Can you think of anything more boring than spending your life weaving white sheets? When they were married they moved into the first house of a row of about six, one room upstairs, one down. Lovely. Bedroom and living-room. What more do you want? Until my cousin Harry came along. So they bought next door – or rented it for about one and six a week. Then they had a kitchen, where they lived, a front room and two bedrooms, Harry's and theirs. Then Cousin Glenda came along, didn't she? So they bought the next one. Now Harry had a bedroom, Glenda had a bedroom, and they had their bedroom. But now they had a spare downstairs room.

So then they turned number-one-house front room into a shop. Number two house became the living-room. Number three house became the kitchen. Later, when Uncle Bert, my Dad's youngest brother, took it all over, number three became the bakehouse, because he was a baker. My Uncle Bert used to make the best brandy snaps in the world. And his daughter Joan made my wedding cake – the first wedding cake she'd ever made.

In those days the Hird family were all a bit noted for their potted meat: Hird's Famous Potted Meat. It was made with best steak. I've seen it minced, and then put in basins and covered with a linen cloth. Auntie Alice had it in her window in her shop in Oldham, and Auntie Clara had it in her window in Walsden, in the middle of tapes, aspirins and everything. The mill workers would come in on their way to work, with their own two slices of bread, and they'd say, 'Two ounces of potted meat.' She'd cut a slice and put it between their two pieces bread, in a bit of paper, and that was their dinner.

In the Hollings pub in Walsden, in the corner, there was a mug with 'Jimmy Hird' on it – my father's pint mug. A right old-fashioned pub pot, for beer. Not a glass tankard. A pot tankard. Perhaps it's still there? It was still there when I was there last time, but that's many years ago. I went to stay at my Auntie Clara's when Jimmy went in the RAF and my Uncle Bert said to me, 'You know, your Dad's pot is still there?'

As soon as I went in, they said, 'Are you Jimmy Hird's girl? Now then, love, have you come to see your Dad's mug?'

Then they were saying, 'And that's Jimmy Shuttleworth's. Do you remember him? Aye, well, he's been gone a bit. That's Ernie so and so's.'

They were very proud of these mugs. It all seems like another world now.

★　★　★

I've been going for fourteen years to the same hotel in Huddersfield. There's always a vase of flowers in my room, and a bowl of fresh fruit. Jane usually stays at Kathy's and they go home together each night. We all call Kathy 'Nora' on the set. Sarah Thomas, who plays my daughter, has the room next to mine. We do our words together, after dinner.

Now my table – why they call it 'my' table I do not know – Sarah sits here, and 'Pearl' sits there. It's the same script every dinner-time:

'Do you mind if I sit here with you, my darling?'

'No, sit down.'

'You're not going to smoke, are you?' says Sarah.

'It's not your table, is it?' Then Pearl finishes the first course, and she'll jump up and say, 'Oh, just excuse me, I've something to do at the desk.'

Sarah says, 'No, you haven't. You're going to have a cigarette.'

'Well, and what if I am?'

I know this script backwards – every night we have it.

'How much are they a packet now?'

'You know very well they are £3.60.'

'They're not! And how many do you smoke a day?'

'Two packets. Anything else you want to know?'

'No, but I mean that's £7.20 a day, so a week that's seven sevens are forty-nine . . .'

'Don't reckon it up! I know.'

And they get quite heated until I say, 'Would you

mind? Everybody's looking at us. Go and have your fag and then come back.'

'Well, she started it.'

The only other one to smoke is Jean Ferguson, 'Marina'. Jean will come to the dinner table. She immediately gets out her cigarettes and looks at me – 'Do you mind?'

I say, 'No.'

'Well, I mind!' – this is Sarah. She says to me later, 'I mean you could say, if you wanted, "no smoking at my table."'

I said, 'Yes, I could if I wanted. I don't want. If they know we're as against smoking as much as we are, they wouldn't ask to sit at our table. And I like them.'

Jean put on a one-woman show about Hylda Baker, which went into the West End, at the Vaudeville Theatre. I went to see it. It was very good – she was excellent. But it was three years of non-stop talking about Hylda Baker.

'Am I talking about her too much?'

'Yes!' we'd all chorus.

'No, but there was just this time when she was at school and . . .'

In the 1999 series Dora Bryan joined the cast. She looked so pretty in the show, playing my younger sister. I don't know how old she is, but she doesn't look her age. There used to be a time when, if there was a maid in a film in England, it was either Esme Cannon or Dora Bryan or me. Dora became a huge star. She was the lead in *Hello, Dolly* in England. She could do the splits, high kicks, everything.

In one scene we did together for *Summer Wine*, we're in the cemetery, at our mother's grave, and she has put an expensive arrangement of flowers – roses and lilies – on the grave, and then they wheel me in with my bunch of Michaelmas daisies. I see these and I see hers.

Then I say, 'You never bought her that many when she was alive.'

So at 'my' table in the evenings we had Nola (my companion), Sarah (no smoking), Dora (has it got any milk in it?), Jean and Thora. Peter and Frank sit together at another table, and might just wave hello to me. But they aren't ever what you might call 'pally'.

Every night Dora would say, 'Now I can't have anything with any milk or cream in it. What is this gravy made of?'

And Paul, the waiter would say, 'Well . . . it's the juice from the meat, a little wine . . .'

'No milk?'

'No. No milk in gravy for beef.'

And then there were the salads. 'No, I don't want any of that because there'll be something in it I shouldn't have.'

It was nearly a variety show. But bless her, she has a warm heart, and I like her very much. Her husband goes with her on tour these days, with the dog. They are both madly in love with this dog. She was telling me,

'No, you see, in the hotel we were in the other week, they said, "No dogs in the restaurant."

'I told them, "But he's very well behaved."

'The head waiter came up and said, "I'm very sorry about this, Mrs Jackson, but it's our policy – no dogs in the restaurant."

'"No? Well, you're not having me, then. Watch how well he behaves, how good he is. 'Sit!'" ' And Thora, he sat there, under the table, good as gold.'

'For how long?'

'Well, just until the head waiter had gone,' she said.

January 1999

8 January Interview Nola Jones-Ransom

A very important person in my life who I haven't yet introduced you to properly is Nola, my admirable companion and Girl Friday and just about everything. Nola is a wonder. She knows where everything is. As I've said, my desk is like a car boot sale, but she can put her hands on anything I want in a second. She used to be in the business herself, so she can come with me to any dinners or functions in the evenings, to help with my chair, and she's so easy and friendly that she fits in with all the people she meets. She's going back to New Zealand in November, and I don't know what I'll do without her.

171

Not in the Diary

Nola comes to Huddersfield with me when we're filming *Summer Wine*. If I get any time off, we like to go round Huddersfield Market. I don't know if you know of a 'moustache cup'? Have you ever heard of one? Are you old enough? Well, I've got one from there. When I was a little girl, Mr Maxwell opposite, Mr Holton and all the men in Morecambe all had moustache cups, because they all had moustaches. A moustache cup has a piece of china across the top, so there's only that half open, and there's a spout and they drink from it with their moustache resting on the top, so they don't get it wet. I haven't seen one since I was a little girl.

Nola and I went to Huddersfield Outside Market. And there on this stall was a moustache cup. I said to the woman, 'How much is that, please?'

And she said, 'Well, never mind how much it is, it's yours, if you want it.'

And I said, 'Well, you'll never retire at that rate, will you?'

She said, 'I'm not wanting to retire.' Then she said, 'It's an invalid cup . . .'

I said, 'No it isn't, love. It's a moustache cup. But you're probably not old enough.'

I went to another stall, where the man had taken my photograph when I was a bit further off, because everywhere I went it was, 'Oh, eh! Is it Thora?'

I said, 'Oh, you do have some nice stuff.'

And he asked, 'What would you say was the nicest thing on this stall?'

I said, 'Well . . . Why?'

And he said, 'Because it's yours.'

(I'm beginning to feel a bit like Queen Mary by now, being given all this free stuff!)

At the covered market there are rows of shops with all open fronts. Last year I saw this champagne-coloured top, fine wool, with rows of tiny pearls. 'Hello, Thora!' (This is what comes from the back of the stall.)

I said, 'Hello, love.'

I saw it was £6. I thought, 'This is ridiculous!' So I said, 'It says "2" on this – what size is that?'

She said, 'What size are you?'

I said, 'Well, floppy . . . 18. Not so floppy . . . 16.'

'Hold on. Here.' She pulls her jumper off – there are other customers there – puts the top on, and says, 'How does that look? I'm a 16.'

I said, 'Well, I'll take it.'

She said, 'We'll knock a pound off. That will be £5.'

Next time I'm up, we pass the shop again. 'Hello, Thora!'

'Hello, love.'

She says, 'Hey! Hey, come in here in a minute.'

'What?'

'We've a pale blue one, like the one you got before.' So she shows me the pale blue one. It was the same size, but she's pulling off her top. I said, 'Nay, don't take your blouse off again . . .'

It was £4. I went out to dinner in the expensive one, the £5 one, on a canal barge the other night and nearly everybody said, 'What a lovely sweater!'

I was sitting next to a man who said he was an admiral. I thought he was joking, because we were on a boat, so I kept making fun. It turned out he really was an admiral.

I've thirty-two pairs of slacks at home. But at another stall they had some nice white ones. I said, 'How much are these?'

The madam who owns it says, '£7.50.'

I said, 'Oh, no. Don't be silly.'

She said, 'Yes, they are. Is your size there?'

So I tell her my size and she looks through and she says, 'No, but I'll have it in tomorrow.'

So the following day I am writing some letters in my room, because I always have to take a portable office up to Huddersfield with me. Nola says, 'Shall I go?' She comes back with a pair of white, a pair of navy and a pair of black slacks. They all fit me. And they are well cut. Three pairs of slacks for £24 – can you believe it?

There was one stall, with 'nothing more than £1.' I bought six beautiful dusters for £1. Five beautiful dish-cloths. The girl said, 'Is there anything else, Miss Hird?'

I said, 'Well, I don't know . . . Wait a minute. What about these floating candles?'

'Eight for £1.' Well, they are 30p each in London. So I had those. And a piece of cardboard with two pairs of tweezers, a pair of scissors, a pair of things to put your nails in to varnish them – £1.

Jan doesn't like rubbish, and now tells me, 'Don't

bring me any more rubbish back. I've been throwing stuff away for ages.'

Right. On this same stall there were some photograph frames that open, in leather, for £1. I showed her the one that I'd got. She said, 'Oh, that is nice.'

I said, 'Would you like one?'

She said, 'I would.' So I bought her two, £1 each. You can't believe it.

A woman stopped me near Marble Arch one day to say, 'Why do you always shout at Wesley, that husband of yours? I do think he's nice.'

I said, 'Oh, do you? Splendid.'

'No, but you're always shouting at him, aren't you?'

I said, 'Well, I suppose . . .'

'I know. I've got one just like him at home . . . But why do you get so cross with him?'

'Only because it's in the script – which I don't write.'

'No, but you do shout at him . . . I mean, why do you shout at him so much?'

She wasn't going to stop arguing about it. So in the end I said, 'Because he's bloody daft. That's why. Good-day to you.'

But as a matter of fact, I have complained to Alan about how nasty my character is. I hate Edie, hate the part sometimes. I don't know why she has to be so rotten. On the other hand, she has given me the chance to put in some bits of my own, memories of my own mother and other northern women, like the business of putting down the newspapers on the clean floor. And people identify with her. The number of people who have stopped me and said, 'Oh, my mother always used to do that.'

Songs of Praise

May 1997

Roger Royle is a professional friend who has become a real friend. He's one of the people who come regularly to the mews to see me for a coffee or tea. We always have a good laugh. Since he left off doing *Songs of Praise* and I stopped doing *Praise Be!* we've sometimes done a little double act together, for charity, in different churches. Well, we've done it together twice to be exact, but it was a great success both times. We've discovered that lots of churches put on their own Songs of Praise, without waiting for the BBC to come along and put it on television. I think they probably have a lot more fun that way. And so Roger does all the interviews with local people, who choose their favourite hymns and then I come along as the star guest, and choose mine.

We don't have a script. We're rather good 'off the cuff', if I say so myself. I think we're better 'off the cuff' than learning a script. He may ask me about my religion, as he has a dog-collar, or about anything really. And he's a very entertaining, witty man himself. I say the normal things about people and faith like the things I said on *Praise Be!* Sometimes he asks me something and I say, 'I shan't tell you that.'

The first time was two or three years ago, at a church in Mill Hill, with the Hendon Band of the Salvation Army, for a *Songs of Praise* in connection with John Grooms Association for Disabled People.

How it came about was this. Just a few weeks before Roger and I had been to the Chelsea Flower Show. As our taxi drew up, a chauffeured Rolls-Royce drew up at the same moment, and two friends of Roger got out and, after we'd been introduced and chatted for a bit, they asked us both to dinner that night. At the Chelsea Flower Show, Roger pushed me round in my wheelchair and we stopped to talk to the members of an excellent Nat West band who were playing. Not as good as a Salvation Army band, but very good. There's nobody really like it, when those girls get their tambourines going.

That evening we went to dinner with his friends, and they asked me to come along to take part in the John Grooms *Songs of Praise*. I've supported John Grooms for years, so of course I said, 'Yes.'

The Rolls-Royce with the chauffeur came to take us both there. There were lots of the John Grooms people in wheelchairs, so I was one of them, you know. It was beautifully organised, and we had a lovely buffet supper afterwards. Roger said, 'I think we did that rather well.' And I thought so, too.

The second occasion was during Lent, the following year. The Parish Church of Kingston-upon-Thames was holding a series of lunch-time interviews. The minister, who was about four foot nine, came bustling into the vestry where we were getting ready and he said, 'It's the first bloody time the church has been full since I've worked here.'

I said, 'What have you just said?'

'Well, I'm not in the sanctuary in this bit. That's the sanctuary just there.'

We did our usual double act, and for the first half Roger interviewed me, and then for the last ten minutes anyone could ask questions – which it felt as though nearly everyone there did.

It was approaching Mothering Sunday weekend, and when we were leaving I spotted a Thornton's chocolate shop just near where Roger had parked the car. I decided to pop in and buy some chocolates for Jan. Roger and I found ourselves having to give a repeat performance, as the shop came to a standstill. I am so lucky that people seem so genuinely pleased to see me. I often think I don't deserve it.

I remember on another occasion I went to a church in Richmond and told them the true story of a Christian artist who had an exhibition of his pictures, beautiful watercolours, all round the walls of the church. Some of them were of Morecambe, and they were all of beautiful places in Britain.

The artist had been a POW in Germany during the Second World War, and he wanted to escape. Another man wanted to escape with him, but he knew that would slow him down. But because he was a Christian he couldn't say, 'No, not you, because we'll be found.' So he took him with him. He had managed to arrange for two sets of workmen's clothes to be left for them, and eventually they did escape and reached occupied France. But by this time they were starving. They hadn't eaten for days, and they were nearly finished. Suddenly they came to a convent. They went to the door, rang the bell, and a very young girl, a novice, came to the door and said, 'Yes, what is it?'

They said, 'We're English.'

She said, 'Come in.'

The sisters in the convent fed them, and they stayed there for a few days until they were well enough to move on, and eventually they got back to England.

Years later he took his wife to France and went to look for the convent. They found it, and the mother superior greeted them and she asked them to a meal, and while they were talking she said, 'Yes, but you've met me before.' The young girl who had let him in was still there, only now she was the mother superior.

The artist sold about £4,000 worth of paintings that day, through my talking about him – all for charity. We went back to his house for lunch afterwards, and his wife, a dear woman, gave us a meal like they would have eaten in this convent.

Even when I was working on *Praise Be!*, the hymn programme, for seventeen years, I never pretended I could actually sing the hymns. My mother had a beautiful voice, but it seems to have bypassed me completely. My grandchildren both sing beautifully, and although I know everyone will think it's because of their father, Mel Tormé, I like to think that it's also something they've got from their great-grandmother. Who knows?

Years ago when I was a little girl there used to be a musical festival every year in Morecambe, and it was a very big one; I think it was one of the biggest in the country. It was held at the Tower, and the competitions were for children from eight to twelve, then twelve to fourteen, fourteen to sixteen and so on. My mother had a great desire for me to be a singer, because she was a singer herself. She sang 'I know that my Redeemer liveth' for seventeen years in the choir at the Wesley Chapel. So I had a singing master and mistress, Mr and Mrs Cooper; he was a talented musician, a very good accompanist and she was a wonderful singer.

We had a girl in Morecambe called Bessie Morphet, who was about ten with a beautiful voice, like Charlotte Church, the little Welsh girl you see on television now. I've got to be honest – I never was a singer. It was just my mother, wishing it. But anyhow, they entered me into the competition when I was about nine. The piece the eight to ten-year-olds had to sing was 'The bailiff's daughter of Islington':

Oh, there was a youth, and a well-beloved youth,
And he was the squire's son,
He loved the bailiff's daughter dear,
Who lived in Islington.

(It's a good story, you see. He's sent away to forget her, and doesn't see her for years. I can't remember what happens in the end – go and get a copy if you want to know!)

So I go in for the musical festival. And Mr Walford Davies – he wasn't Sir Walford then – was the adjudicator. He would come on the stage with all his papers after all the singers had done their turn and make his remarks. If they were any good you could pay sixpence and go to Morecambe Town Hall the following day and get a copy. I think we all knew that Bessie would win easily. I was sitting with my mother. I think I was number forty-three to sing, so we had a long time to wait until he came to me. And it's funny how you remember words absolutely as they were spoken. He stood there and he said, 'Forty-three. Yes. Now number forty-three . . . Well, let us be very fair about this. She will never be a great singer . . . but, oh, what an actress!' I think I came about twenty-third. But at least I was mentioned in dispatches.

Now the following year the competition was at Lytham

St Anne's, outside Blackpool. And what do you think the competition song was? 'I attempt from love's sickness to fly'. Imagine asking a child of ten or eleven to sing that.

I attempt from love's sickness to fl-y-y-y-y-y-y in vain.
Since I am myself my own fever,
Since I am myself my own fever and pain.
No more, now, no more, with pride, dear heart,
     do not swell.
I cannot raise forces, I cannot raise forces enough
     to rebel . . .

I didn't know what the hell I was singing about. I was nearly the bottom of the thing that time. I think I must have been so rotten, they didn't even mention me in the adjudication.

Now as I've said, I have a most lovable little dresser on *Summer Wine* called Jenny Snape. She is such a bonny, attractive young woman. (It's her son who was the young boy in *The Full Monty* that I gave the award to.) And when she was dressing me on the last series I heard her humming under her breath, 'There was a youth, and a well-beloved youth' so, of course, I joined in.

Then we both said, 'How did you know that?' She said she'd sung it at school.

So every morning after that, she and I sang 'The bailiff's daughter of Islington' while she got me dressed as Edie. And I thought, 'How funny – from one end of your life to the other, to find that song.'

⋆ ⋆ ⋆

I don't have my own programme any more, but I still get asked to be on other religious programmes on radio and television. I did a special programme for Christmas Day 1999, talking to John Stapleton and choosing my favourite carols. I spoke about Lyngham – the tune that I think is the right one for 'While shepherds watched' ever since the Salvation Army used to play it in Cheapside, Morecambe, each Christmas morning when I was a child.

Two girls from the unit who came to help me prepare it all were so nice, so polite, so able. They came round to see me many times. They would telephone and say, 'Can we have half an hour?'

And I'd say, 'Come round for a coffee.'

So it was a pleasure to do. They took a suite at the Royal Lancaster for the recording. I gave them a big box of photographs and I said to them, 'Don't lose *one* of these, because every one is precious.' So it will be nice for me to see that on the television at Christmas.

And I've been on the *Heaven and Earth Show*. The one with the cook. I talked about the hymns I like, and my religion. I always talk the same way about my religion. I said to them, 'Hold on, before we do it. What I'm saying, I've said it all before.'

'Ah, well, but not on our programme you haven't, you see.'

I always say that my assistance from God is so great that it takes quite a bit to thank him each evening, because there are so many things during the day he helps me with. And that I must have been a Christian since I was little, and didn't know it. I always tell about Uncle Robert. I had four uncles, my mother's brothers, all fishermen for shrimps, and then Uncle Robert had to stop, because he had rheumatism. Any pain in your bones in the old days was rheumatism. There was no neuritis, no arthritis, no anything. Just rheumatism.

I can see him in our kitchen as though it was now. Black curly hair sprinkled with grey. Peaked cap with the leather peak. And the point of the story is – a neighbour came in to borrow something from my mother and saw him and said, 'By God, Robert, you do look like Jesus.' And for years after that I thought not that Uncle Robert looked like Jesus, but that Jesus looked like my Uncle Robert. Then when I was about eleven I went through a rather serious phase, and I began to worry that I was being a bit disrespectful, thinking that. So I said to my mother, when she came up to hear me say my prayers, 'Jesus doesn't really look like my Uncle Robert, does he?'

To which my wonderful mother, taking my face in her hands and looking at me most lovingly, replied, 'Who says he doesn't?'

I've always had the same idea of heaven since I was a little girl. There are a lot of flowers, and it's very beautiful all year round, never like a winter down here, when the flowers are dead. So many people I love are there already. Surely one or two of them will wait and meet me. I rather picture them in white, I don't know why. When I say my prayers at night, I always picture my sister in a long white dress. And my mother.

It's like a little encampment. Jimmy and his mother and father and sisters are all there together. My brother and sister, my mother and father. And my best friend, Brenda, who has recently died of cancer. She was an only child, and her mother and father, I see them all there. They always smile a bit when I picture them when I'm saying my prayers at night.

Scottie and I loved each other very dearly. But when he'd had his massive stroke he didn't know us – well, he didn't *anything*, that's all I can say; it wasn't that he didn't know us. Jan and I went to see him every day for a week. We had been with him all day on the Saturday, and when I got home I sat on my bed and said to God, 'Oh, will you take him while he's asleep?' That was seven o'clock. At two in the morning the hospital rang to say that he'd died – in his sleep. Jan was with me at the mews, and answered the telephone. She came into my bedroom and said, 'Mummy, Daddy's free.'

People sometimes ask me if I'm glad I did *Praise Be!* for all those years. Glad? Oh! I think of the year I began in the garden, when all the ducks waddled past me. And another time I told the audience about Jan's mallard, who came every year to build her nest, and used to look round the grounds like someone looking for a new house. Then I said, 'Now I know you're all interested in the duck, because we're getting some letters, but we can't find her. But if we find her in the course of the next seven weeks, we'll let you know.'

And we did find her. Outside the dining-room door was this rose bush, and there she was, hidden under it. And I said to the team, 'We've found the nest – and nine baby ducklings!' ·

And the producer said, 'Well, you say about it.'

So I talked to the audience. I said, 'We've got some lovely news – we've found the duck – nine babies! Could you come this way, camera, please?' You know, it was very American, the whole idea, and the camera followed me, and we looked down. And I said, 'See how well she's hidden them.' And everyone saw these tiny bits of fluff.

It was so great, that place at Isfield. And I told Jan's dogs the story of St Francis, with three biscuits on the floor, and the dogs all acting as though they were listening to me, when they were just waiting to be told they could eat their biscuits, with Jan behind the camera.

Glad? Was it Norfolk we went where the nuns were? And there was a statue of St Francis. And the baby lambs, and all the chickens. I remember the young sister running after them, in Marks and Spencer tights. I couldn't get over the mother superior there being so young and her name was Pamela. She still writes. We write to each other about twice a year.

Glad? It was really a wonderful programme to be in, and if you were even slightly religious, the joy was greater. And the things that happened, like the man who said, 'I think you're wonderful, I think the programme's wonderful, but I wish you wouldn't wear nail varnish.'

And I said, 'It's coming off. Let's please everybody.'

Remember me telling the story about the man behind the rock for 'Rock of ages'? We used to find stories of where the hymns had been written. And we went to where the minister had written 'Onward Christian soldiers' for the children to march to. And we showed the street they would have marched along. And don't think I'm looking for work – but if you could hear the number of people who still stop me and say, 'You aren't doing the hymns now, are you?'

I've often thought – we were a team, that made *Praise Be!* It wasn't just me, it was the producer and the director and all the invisible people – the crew. Do you know, we did it for seventeen years, and for most of those years we always had the same cameraman and sound man and even the same autocue operator, Jeremy. Because they all put their names to come back each year to Jan and William's home in Sussex where we filmed it.

They told me it had wonderful viewing figures. I think it was because we've always put a lot of laughing in our work, but were serious when we did it, that's why we've got anywhere. I think you've got to be serious when you are doing it, think the right things the first two or three times, and then enjoy it. Do you follow? Religion is serious, but you have to laugh to show how serious it is. Comedy is funny, but you have to be serious to make it funny. Working for seventeen years on a programme like

Praise Be! changed my life. God had always been a part of my life, since I was a little girl, but I hadn't always remembered how thankful I was for all the blessings of my life. Now I never go to sleep without thanking the Lord. Yes. I am glad I did *Praise Be!*

November 1999

27 November – Broadcasting House Radio Theatre
'An Evening with Thora Hird'

Well, here I am, travelling at a snail's pace through the Christmas shopping traffic in the West End of London to Broadcasting House. 'Thou shalt be punctual' is my eleventh commandment, and I'm glad I insisted that we set off really early. I am expected in the famous Concert Hall in the heart of that familiar building in Langham Place, to make my first contribution to television for the year 2000 – even though I haven't opened the first window of my Advent Calendar for 1999 yet. Television producers are always a season ahead – they probably made nearly all the shows for this Christmas last summer.

Actually this is my second visit to the beautifully restored Concert Hall in Broadcasting House, which has been the setting for years of so many favourite radio comedy shows. Last week all of us on *Summer Wine* came here to remember Bill Owen.

Not in the Diary

★ ★ ★

The above was what I was thinking about in the limousine taking me to Broadcasting House for a special edition for *Songs of Praise*. It was done with an invited audience from all my favourite charities – the Stroke Association, John Grooms, the Ancient Order of Foresters, Help the Aged – and Dorothy Crisp brought along some of the men from the Star and Garter. Pam Rhodes interviewed me, and there was a Salvation Army quintet to accompany some of my favourite hymns. Members of the team who had worked with me on *Praise Be!* came along, and some more good old friends gave video messages, like they do on *This is Your Life*. It was great to see Harry Secombe, looking 100 per cent better after his stroke, and he not only sent a message, he sang 'Abide with Me' for me. Larry Adler reprieved his mouth-organ version of 'Onward Christian soldiers', and the Archbishop of York appeared on the screen to wish me well. So it was a lovely evening – lots of happy memories and favourite hymns.

The only problem was getting in. The car delivered me at Broadcasting House in Langham Place, where the BBC commissionaires all greeted me warmly and were delighted to see me. The *Songs of Praise* producer, Sian Salt, was there with Pam Rhodes to meet me, and I was accompanied by Felix, my agent, and my friends Andrew and Liz Barr, who work for the BBC in Edinburgh, and everyone was charming. Then Liz started to push my wheelchair through the turnstyle to get me to the radio

190

theatre where we were recording the programme. The BBC commissionaires all froze like statues, and then barred our way.

'You aren't going through there, are you?' they said.

I said, 'Well, unless you want me to do it out in the hallway, yes, I am.'

'You can't go through there.'

The producer said, 'But Dame Thora is invited here – it has all been arranged. She's taking part in the programme.'

I said, 'If I can't go through, that's all right, we'll go to the pictures, and you can do the programme without me.'

Do you know, after all that smiling welcome, they would not let us through, even accompanied by the producer, without making us wait for special passes that we had to pin to ourselves? Can you believe it? They said it was for 'Security'.

I said, 'Do you think I'm a spy, or something?' Whatever is the world coming to?

There was another pantomime when we did get through to the back, because the stage, and even more importantly, the loo, were up and down a flight of stairs from my dressing-room – where I will say there was champagne and chocolates and vanilla slice all laid out for me. There was a chairlift to get you over this hump of stairs – but, believe it or not, nobody knew how to work it. First there was one, then two, then four commissionaires all saying to one another, 'Do you know how to work this?'

'No, I don't. I think it needs two keys.'

In the end about six commissionaires were trying this lever and that lever, but they couldn't get it to start. They got as far as getting me onto it, but then I was stranded there. Roger Royle arrived while all this was going on, and I thought he was going to fall down on the floor laughing.

That's the trouble with show business – even when you are doing things for the Lord, it can still all go wrong. But in the end it was all beautiful. The audience were all so loving, and it was like being back on *Praise Be!* for an evening.

7 December

Rehearse 'Mary'

Tony Robinson has written a five-minute monologue for me to play Mary, the Mother of Jesus, for the last Christmas of the millennium. I never thought I'd be starring in a nativity play at eighty-eight! This time it's about Mary as an old lady, remembering the first Christmas, and the sadness of the crucifixion, and now she's waiting for her Son to come and take her home.

But it is set in modern times, so she's in an old folks' home, like any old lady waiting for her son to come and visit her. Well, you may have seen it before you read this book, but as I write, it's still just a date in my diary

– rehearse 7 December, record 16 December, transmission: Christmas Day.

Christmas Day 1999

I shall be spending Christmas with Jan at Bailiffscourt, a lovely old-fashioned hotel near Littlehampton. There's a big four-poster bed and a log fire in the bedroom. A choir will come in and sing carols for us on Christmas Eve (not in the bedroom, of course) and then the hotel provides transport to the village church for Midnight Mass. They have also promised that Christmas Day lunch will be over in time for the Queen's Speech. William will be over in the States seeing his children and staying with his sister, who would otherwise be alone this year. They are both very good – keeping everybody happy!

New Year's Eve

The New Year will be spent quietly with Jan and William in Chichester, visiting Chichester Cathedral in the morning, and watching television in the evening. I might even go to bed before midnight!